Noah's Ark

Bruce Weiss

authorHOUSE®

AuthorHouse™
1663 Liberty Drive
Bloomington, IN 47403
www.authorhouse.com
Phone: 833-262-8899

No part of this book may be reproduced, stored in a retrieval system, or transmitted by any means without the written permission of the author.

Published by AuthorHouse 07/20/2020

ISBN: 978-1-7283-6710-1 (sc)
ISBN: 978-1-7283-6711-8 (hc)
ISBN: 978-1-7283-6709-5 (e)

Library of Congress Control Number: 2020913075

Print information available on the last page.

Any people depicted in stock imagery provided by Getty Images are models, and such images are being used for illustrative purposes only. Certain stock imagery © Getty Images.

This book is printed on acid-free paper.

Because of the dynamic nature of the Internet, any web addresses or links contained in this book may have changed since publication and may no longer be valid. The views expressed in this work are solely those of the author and do not necessarily reflect the views of the publisher, and the publisher hereby disclaims any responsibility for them.

Introduction

"It was granted for me for many years to live and work under the greatest son whom my nation has brought forth in the thousand years of its history. Even if I could I would not expunge this period from my existence. I regret nothing. If I were standing once more at the beginning I should act once again as I did then, even if I knew that at the end, I should be burned at the stake….." Rudolf Hess

PART ONE

CHAPTER ONE

September 1987

The sound of the impact could be heard miles away. Theo's wife Sara age thirty eight and son Blake age fourteen were killed on their way home from the local movie theater. It was a perfect day for a movie, cold with heavy rain on an early fall afternoon. Their late model SUV had been struck broadside at an intersection, the traffic signals not functioning due to the storm's intensity. The responding EMTS wrote in their report there was nothing that could be done for the victims.

Son Noah and Theo were home when the police arrived. With ominous looks and somber tones they informed Theo there had been an accident involving two vehicles downtown. The words were terse and uttered in halting sentences, the officers looking ghastly. The sorrowful explanation was his wife and child were in one of the cars. There were no survivors. It felt as if the sky had suddenly crashed down, a cold and foreboding feeling suffocating Theo. When the realization hit harder he fell to his knees, shocked and bewildered. It couldn't be his wife and child he prayed, but his prayer would not be answered.

Holding son Noah's hand, a precocious loving child of eleven Theo could not find words to console him. A hug sufficed for the moment, an embrace so strong the boy gasped for air. One of the officers put his arms around them asking if he might say a prayer. Heart palpitations and light headedness added to his distress. Nothing in life would ever be the same again he realized, the old life over. Noah with hazel green eyes like his mother seemed frozen, his young life obviously in great peril.

A fifth grader, Noah was talented and outgoing until the words about the catastrophe broke him. When the officers left the house the boy simply shut down, unable or possibly just unwilling to utter a single word. His eyes were blank, the expression unreadable. Theo curled his fingers through Noah's dark hair seeing no outward reaction.

Hours turned into dreary days and bleak nights filled with alarming nightmares. Noah had not spoken a single word since the tragedy, possibly his way of grieving Theo suspected. The first week passed in eerie silence.

Theo sought professional help not for himself but for Noah who remained completely mute but nothing seem to help the boy abandon his silent world. 'It's a child's worst nightmare when a mother dies' one therapist explained. Theo was cautioned not to force Noah to share feelings or what he was thinking. Most children revert to speech after trauma when they are ready another child psychologist related.

Seven unsettled weeks passed until the day Noah's school principal called saying the boy was falling far behind the others. Alternate schooling was advised. Theo suspected as much, already decided on home schooling.

Long curly black hair cascaded beneath the beret Noah always wore, the silence growing more deafening every day. No matter what Theo said or did nothing penetrated Noah's silent world. Weeks after the accident Theo declared the days of home schooling lessons were over. Weeks of trying to remain upbeat and calm wore him out, dread and loss sapping the tiny bits of hope and strength he kindled.

Saying over and over they were a team, always together and best friends and partners he grew tired of his own voice. We'll get through this became the daily mantra, the heartbreaking new life after the tragedy growing more and more unbearable each day. Theo doubted they'd ever be a normal healthy family again.

Emphasizing good and positive things had no effect. There was a dying ember inside Noah he sensed, hopeful it would re-ignite life inside Noah's empty shell. The child showed little emotion as if he were a million miles away. Theo took solace crying at night when Noah was asleep, feeling quite fragile. One therapist said there would be no future if the past wasn't properly dealt with. Theo wanted to jump up and strangle her.

After another failed doctor's appointment Theo declared the home lessons were officially ended. Closing the math book he told Noah he'd been thinking about something very special for them. With a smile and wink he said he'd been working out a geographical cure for their troubles, that it was a good time to put some of the sadness and sorrow aside. Fleeing was not an option one therapist insisted but Theo thought different. It would not be a cure-all but he'd try anything. As usual Noah had no reaction, as if he hadn't heard the words.

Would uprooting Noah from his home do more harm than good? Reading Noah's reactions was impossible save for a slight movement of the head. "Come on over to the couch and sit by me. I want to show you something."

Scooping up a large dog eared carton Theo announced it was filled with old photographs and letters passed down by relatives on the Scottish McCann side of the family. "This carton contains treasures Noah, putting a tiny look of wonder on the boy's face, barely perceptible.

Long forgotten in the attic the carton sat unopened for nearly fifteen years. Theo told about the first time he'd discovered it. The old cardboard smelled moldy, the scent of old burned Scottish peat embedded.

"I want to share these photographs and letters with you and I'll even let you read some of the letters if you'd like." Theo held onto a tiny thread of hope that when he began to read the letters aloud he might get a reaction.

"I have a wonderful story to tell you about our ancestors so I'm going to let you to stay up later than usual. The story of our family begins with a man by the name of James McCann, a distant relative, a Scottish farmer.

He lived to the ripe old age of one hundred. I'm descended from him and you are too."

He held up an old faded sepia picture of a man identified as one of James great grandsons. Theo smiled when Noah drew his finger across the man's long white beard. With the same motion Noah ran his finger over Theo's face.

"James was a farmer in a tiny Scottish village called Eaglesham, not terribly far from the border with England. Would you like to hear about the village where our ancestors came from?" There was no response.

In the weeks since the tragedy Theo had to continually remind himself there could be no scolding or admonishment, counting to ten often saving grace. The few times the anger became too obvious tears ran down Noah's cheeks.

"The town records tell us a lot about the McCann's who first settled in the village in the year 1746." Showing Noah faded copies of original land deeds, Theo asked if he could read the ancient scrawl. The boy had no response.

"The McCann family owned nearly 100 square acres of farm land, about five hundred times larger than our lawn here. James and brother Samuel and Samuel's wife Elizabeth built a home made out of stone on that land, a home for generations to come. Somewhere in this carton there are a couple of letters passed down through the years and if you trace the history of the family it eventually leads to you and me. Their daily life was very different from the way we live Noah. Imagine no electricity, no phone, no indoor toilets, no refrigerator, no cars; practically nothing we have today.

"This letter was written by Samuel's brother, your great, great, great uncle Max asking permission to clear forest land in order to create more grazing area for sheep. This note is from his wife's sister Elizabeth explaining the need for more adventurous people moving to Eaglesham in order to create a small market area. Elizabeth left behind her diary, much of the wording devoted to the time the town began establishing a handloom weaving industry. Her hope was it might bring hard currency in, meaning money."

There was no discernable reaction from Noah so Theo pressed on.

"Great great grandfather Owen McCann created the first street plan for the village in the early 1800's. Town land records mention that most of the farm land was turning to hard scrabble, meaning land difficult to farm. The reason? Overgrazing by sheep and cattle. Owen vowed to change the farm. His letters describe the problems with the land and his encouragement for weavers, metal smiths, shopkeepers, inn keepers, and wine makers to move to the village.

"Owen's son Richard lived to the ripe old age of ninety-nine. His very thorough accounting books tells of the agricultural products raised and sold on the farm. During his lifetime many people moved away to the industrial city of Glasgow, the population of Eaglesham dwindling to less than two hundred.

"Richard gave his sons heartfelt advice, encouraging them to move to the city or possibly join those moving to America searching for a better future. He continued to maintain the McCann land but it became harder and harder each planting season. There had been McCann's living in the village for nearly two hundred and fifty years but that changed as all things do. The last McCann's living in Eadlesham were Charles, his wife Mary and their three children Angus, Arthur and Sander. In 1929 Sander who'd served in the army remained behind, the rest of the family migrating to America. My parents Carl and Betsy, your grandparents came to America settling in upstate New York where I was born.

"Noah, I've wondered from time to time if there just might be one McCann still living in Scotland on the farm. His name might have been Sander but I can't say if he's still alive."

Pausing he asked Noah if was tired and wanted to go to bed or stay up and hear more about the family. The response was the interminable silence, the most difficult time to hide disappointment. End of story for now he said.

Tucking Noah into bed but instead of a bedtime story, Theo whispered there was one more great surprise he'd kept to himself.

"If you and I were to travel to Scotland, a place very far away we could explore our ancestor's village of Eaglesham. Think of it as the greatest school field trip ever, our days filled with hiking and possibly discovering more about the lives of our ancestors. We can find a nice old inn staying for a few days or as long as we'd like. Sleep on it and we'll talk more about it tomorrow."

It was impossible to ascertain if Noah understood any of the words.

"I'll be reading in the living room so remember just call out if you need me and I'll be there." It took only a second to realize that impossibility. Noah went right to sleep.

In the days leading up to the journey Theo poured through the old diaries and a few recently acquired informational books about Scotland. To his delight if it turned out to be an extended stay, Eaglesham had a primary school, a library and playing fields. As to whether any McCann's might be found that was doubtful but at least they'd be in a place where their families once lived.

Chapter Two

It wasn't a done deal. Theo hesitated booking flights hoping Noah might start talking again any day. Each morning he awoke thinking about the great distance they might travel, hopefully jogging something that might bring Noah back to life. Concerned a geographic cure to escape their misfortune might be a terrible mistake kept him awake some nights. Would the move create more chaos in Noah's silent world he wondered?

Their flights were finally booked, Theo committed to the journey as long as Noah remained silent. Of great concern was Noah's reaction to leaving home, an island protected from life's storms.

Buckling their seatbelts on the airplane Theo eyed the arriving passengers, curious who might take the window seat in their row. One by one fellow passengers strolled by until a woman in a business suit stopped by their row. Stowing her bag in the overhead bin she asked Noah if he might like to sit by the window so he could look out. Without answering Noah moved to the window seat, the women taking the aisle seat. After takeoff and dinner Noah closed his eyes, his head on Theo's lap.

The woman read a magazine as the sky darkened, the cabin lights dimming. No one spoke until Theo asked an innocuous question. Had she ever visited Scotland. Yes she replied, several times to attend medical conferences.

"Are you a doctor Theo asked? She nodded, adding she was on her way to Glasgow to deliver a paper she'd spent some time preparing." Theo offered he was a part time history professor at a community college and a part time at home writer, mostly mysteries and historical fiction. He was on sabbatical he related, taking son Noah hopefully to discover their ancestral roots in a tiny village near Glasgow. Mentioning home schooling he referred to their journey as the ultimate school field trip. Names were exchanged.

The woman introduced herself as Dr. Joan Ark. When he stared a little too long because she was quite comely he felt embarrassed. Possibly late thirty's or early forties he guessed, light complexion and eyes an amazing electric green. She was quite stylish he thought, wearing a gray business suit adorned with silver buttons at the wrist. While she read he studied the laugh lines on her face, not your typical medical doctor he sensed. Looking down he eyed her ankle high laced boots, worn but highly polished.

Asking about her medical field Dr. Joan Ark replied she was a child psychologist focusing on children's anxieties. Theo let out an audible gasp asking if there was one particular childhood anxiety her specialty.

Dr. Ark explained all anxieties had a common denominator but she specialized in one particular trauma. "I work with children who've experienced a terrible tragedy in their young lives, children who've become terribly lost, many who've lose their ability to carry on a normal life. That syndrome usually renders a child unable to express emotion. It's rare but not uncommon after experiencing severe trauma for a child when they become fearful of their own voices. When they can't express themselves with word we apply a medical term which is selective mutism. Have you ever heard of this?"

Theo shook his head no, nearly leaping out of his seat restrained only by the seatbelt. Would it be selfish or insensitive to tell her about Noah's situation he wondered? Staring at his sleeping child he decided it wasn't the right time or place to burden the doctor with his problems. What if Noah awoke and heard their conversation? Whether it was fate or providence it was impossible to quiet the thoughts running through his head. "Would you mind telling me a little about your work," immediately wishing he hadn't asked.

"Aphasia voluntaria' she whispered, is the Latin medical term for someone so thoroughly affected by trauma he or she stops talking. As I said it's rare but there are enough cases to keep me quite busy." Theo was certain she could not know he was dealing with a situation like that with Noah. Never heard the term before he managed to whisper.

"I've studied the inability of children over the age of four to talk, which by the way has nothing to do with will power. A child affected has no control and simply shuts down, the muteness or silence usually occurring during or immediately after a traumatic event. Workers in my field maintain it occurs when a child feels the need to protect him or herself from something they don't have the skill or ability to cope with. A child with muteness was probably once very proficient, vocalizing with family and friends but something very painful changed that. Parents and teachers and friends recognize the immediate negative and devastating effects."

Theo knew he shouldn't relate what happened in their lives; wrong place and wrong time to ask someone to work on their time off. Mercifully Noah slept soundly but before takeoff he hadn't said a word. Did Dr. Ark have suspicions about the boy he wondered, or did she think he was simply painfully shy or sleepy? She probably wanted to get back to her magazine or look over her lecture notes he surmised, telling himself to back off. In a moment of weakness and despair he asked her to tell him more about her work with selective mutism.

"I actually enjoy talking about my work. You'd be surprised how many people respond saying they knew someone who'd experienced those circumstances. We've come a long way in our treatments. Many non-verbal-disorders begin with crying and clinging but to others it's complete silence. Many of the causative traumas I deal with were brought about due to rape, molestation, abuse or certain failing family dynamics. My paper is about children exhibiting anxiety disorders, children who for the most part become suddenly frightened by the sound of their own voice. Social phobias often create a high level of anxiety and for some children it's quite acute."

Is there a cure Theo blurted out, regretting the words, especially if she said no.

"A child's inability to talk interferes with healthy development so it's critical to begin therapy as soon as possible. When a child's inability to talk is not related to physical problems, the child will usually overcome selective mutism in time but only with intense therapy, best done in a residential treatment center. Most children will eventually verbalize their anxieties thus overcoming their inability to talk."

Theo desperately wanted to talk about Noah but was convinced it would be unwise. He wondered however if she might think the conversation more than just an interest in her work. A flight announcement gave Theo a chance to take a deep breath, the kindly doctor returning to her magazine. There was much more he would have loved to say but feigning sleepiness he closed his eyes. There would be no sleep he understood because of an overactive mind. They didn't speak again during the flight but upon landing the two exchanged addresses in Scotland.

Theo felt like a zombie, the old life sadly sucked out of him. Like a vinyl record stuck and unable to play on, the vision of the day the two policemen came to his home delivering the devastating news haunted him.

In the baggage area Dr. Ark reached out taking Noah's hand saying she hoped he would have a grand time in Scotland on his special field trip. Theo felt empty, a great opportunity possibly missed when they went their separate ways. He was dismayed he didn't have the daring to tell her about Noah. Curiously though, Theo sensed Doctor Ark knew somehow what Noah was experiencing.

Away from the airport the rural roads led them to the seaside town of Exeter for the night. Settling into their room Noah pulled his treasured books from his backpack. Theo spent time going over the manuscript he hoped might be turned into his next novel.

There were times the previous weeks when he feared the anger he fought so hard to suppress would suddenly explode with the force of a volcano, certain Noah sensed his dark thoughts.

After a late lunch the two strolled down to the sea for a long walk, collecting shells and beach glass. Theo explained he'd arranged for a ride to Eaglesham late the next morning after a good night's sleep. The long flight and the sea air tired them making for an early dinner and bedtime.

The next morning they were back in the countryside, Theo hoping the dramatic change in scenery might stir life inside Noah. A tiny discernable glimmer in Noah's dark eyes gave Theo the feeling perhaps they were on a good road.

Stopping in a small village for lunch their driver joined them reciting Scottish folk tales. Noah seemed to hang on every word. Reaching their final destination of Eaglesham turned out to be a real eye opener. The village could be something out of the middle ages was Theo's first impression. In bold letters a weathered wooden plaque announced the village was first settled in the year eleven fifty-two. On both sides of the road fields where barley was seasonally harvested had only brown stalks. Flocks of crows flew about the fields chatting noisily. Theo told the driver there seemed to be great harmony between the land and the sky.

Arriving in the main square the place looked uninhabited. Where were all the people Theo wondered, realizing it was Sunday. Spying a large stone building at the far end of the square he observed several elderly women sitting on the steps. It was not the municipal building the driver related but a grand old hotel built in 1852.

The building's gray cut-stone appeared well weathered. Asking the driver to wait Theo went inside checking on availability. Franz the innkeeper said they were to be the only guests at the inn so he would give them the grandest room on the second floor. As to how long they might stay, Theo replied he was uncertain saying a day or two but possibly much longer. Reaching into his pocket to pull out his wallet a card fell out with Dr. Joan Ark's hotel name and number.

Their room was rather quaint, time worn floors and walls of dark heavy oak. Heavy faded purple drapes hung from iron curtain rods, the view the gardens below. The room was sparsely furnished save an impressive oaken armoire and a comfortable sagging sofa. Noah tested the magnificent four poster with a few jumps, a satisfied look on his face. The rock fireplace took up nearly an entire wall, as ancient looking as the outside of the building. Peat bricks stacked neatly near the fireplace would be the only source of heat.

Theo was informed by Franz the town was entirely closed up on Sundays, the reason no one was about. After exchanging pleasantries he and Noah were offered a tour of the building and grounds along with insightful information about the village. Franz insisted they not return any later than eight if they went out because that was when the kitchen closed.

"My wife Greta prepares a very special hunters feast for locals and guests starting at six every Sunday religiously. The menu includes fresh killed boar, pheasant shot this very morning, venison and local trout. All the root vegetables are grown locally."

Strolling carefree about the town Theo told Noah what he'd learned about the McCann family. "If we get very lucky the old homestead where generations of McCann's lived might still be standing, although most likely abandoned." Theo was certain the last of the McCann's were long gone but kept it to himself.

Under a dull chilly gray sky on antique bicycles courtesy of the inn the pair set off on a narrow country lane barely wide enough for a single car. Box lunches in their baskets, courtesy of Greta were welcomed. A town map drawn by Franz sketched the road that would eventually lead them to the oldest original section of the village. "I wonder if we'll find any trace of the old farm family homestead," Theo remarked.

The eternal hope was the journey might somehow stir the silence from Noah. Looking into his dark eyes the only reaction to being away seemed the boy's insatiable curiosity about the plants, birds and insects. Navigating the narrow lane meant listening for the sounds of approaching cars.

Thankfully the only discernable sounds were the insects and birds. Noah looked curiously at the few scattered stone houses and the grand views of the Scottish countryside so different from the States. Fields filled with yellow flowering bramble stretching as far as the eye could see. Several steep hills slowed their journey and at times they walked their bikes. Hedgerows on both sides of the lane hid the sun's warming rays making for a chilly ride. The stone walls were as smooth as a baby's bottom Theo commented. "They've been weathered over the centuries into that dull green mossy gray you see. Let's stop because I want you to touch the moss. It's like touching a cloud."

Noah reached for Theo's hand, something he'd not done for a very long time. The gesture gave Theo more confidence that by the end of their journey Noah might be talking again.

The tiny lane branched only once, the hard pan dirt road heading east called Patience, the other to the west called Hope. "Patience Lane should take us to the old McCann homestead according to the map."

Ten minutes further down the road the stone walls were only half as high and they got their first look at the deep narrow valley where Eaglesham was first settled. Spying acres of gray boulders strewn about, Theo said they were probably the foundation stones of the houses and barns that once flourished, once the hub of the village.

In the middle of the valley one single house stood among the ruins, leaning as if the winds of time had attacked it relentlessly. The area was indeed deserted, ruins of a once prosperous farming community Franz had said. There were no people about and no grazing animals, only the large weathered granite stones. Hoisting Noah on top of the wall to get a better look a flock of birds nestling in the hedgerows nosily took flight.

"Noah, one of those rock piles might have been the home of the McCann's. When we go into the town hall office tomorrow we might hopefully find out. The Scottish kept excellent land records I was told."

Poking around the debris Noah found a place to sit out of the wind to enjoy their picnic lunches. Theo took a number of photos, giving the camera to Noah to take pictures of things that interested him. For the briefest of moments Theo felt peace for the first time in weeks.

CHAPTER THREE

Winding their way back to the inn against a strong wind Theo thought about Dr. Joan Ark's words, especially her knowledge of selective mutism, Was it coincidence or fate or luck for a change that a doctor with knowledge of what Noah was going through would unexpectedly turn up in their lives? What were the odds someone with knowledge of children's traumatic silence would actually sit in the same row of seats on an airplane?

Professional support for Noah had not worked, a waste of time and money leaving Theo disappointed and perplexed. Each new appointment began with hope only to be disappointed each time. Would it be insensitive or tactless to call Dr. Ark's hotel, asking if she might have some time to talk about Noah? The thought created a dull ache in his head, knowing that would be highly intrusive, not to mention possibly getting bad advice. Would the recurring theme of rejection spoil his time away with Noah in Scotland? Trying to put the craziness aside he thought about the banquet, although he wasn't terribly hungry. It turned out however to be a feast to end all feasts.

Waking early the next morning they'd weren't hungry but couldn't wait to partake in what Franz called a hunters breakfast. In store for anther gastronomical adventure they sampled scrumptious exotic morsels prepared in Greta's kitchen.

The weather wasn't great in the morning, everything gray; the sky, the town buildings, the roads, the trees and fields and the few people up and about. Strolling to the old town hall Noah grabbed Theo's hand again.

"What treasures and secrets about the McCann clan might be found behind those heavy looking old doors" Theo said?

The entrance hallway was lined with old black and white faded photographs of the village and it's inhabitants. Theo whispered perhaps one of the photos could be the McCann farm. Hoisting Noah onto his shoulders they made their way down the long hall into a large open room. Fascinated by the collection of photographs Theo didn't hear approaching footsteps. Turning around he spied an elderly man, looking nearly as ancient as the building.

The man sported a long white beard with hair sprouting in every direction under a Scottish tam. A retired professor Theo guessed, a town elder? Sporting muscular arms and calloused hands Theo thought the man had a tough life, possibly a farmer. Most striking were the bushy white eyebrows nearly covering his entire forehead. Maybe an ancient warrior he wondered. Shaking hands the man said welcome to Eaglesham.

"Where are you lads from," asked in a thick Scottish brogue?

"From the United States and we've come to your village to see if we might find information about our ancestors who once lived and worked here. This much I know for certain. The McCann's settled here in the early 1700's.

"What did you say the name of the family was?"

"The McCann's. My name is Theo McCann and this boy is my son Noah. As I said we hope to discover the names of relatives and a little bit about their lives. I'm nearly certain there are no McCann's living here anymore so would you be able to guide us?"

"McCann you say? Why'd you say you're nearly certain there are no McCann's in the village?"

"I just assumed they're all gone for probably a number of reasons. I'm a descendent of the McCann clan, many who migrated to the States at the beginning of the new century. I've got a treasure trove of old letters home in America and some very old photographs as well diaries from years back. I know a bit about the McCann's but I'd like to learn more. The family relics I have were passed down generation to generation, eventually coming to me. From what I've read it's became apparent that the last of the McCann's left the village sometime just after World War Two. That would be my grand parents and parents, sadly no longer alive."

The old gentleman bent down close to Noah asking if he got his name from the Bible. Noah naturally did not answer so Theo answered the boy was very shy. The gentleman nodded.

The old man ran his hand through his full chock of white hair, a large cotton swab came to Theo's mind. Asking if there might be old land records or deeds stored in the town hall, Theo hoped the answer would be yes. "Would any of the land records possibly point to the exact locate of the old McCann homestead?

The question put a large knowing grin on the man's face but no immediate response. The twinkle in his eyes suggested Theo had asked the right question.

"I'll look up the land records for you but first I want to tell you an interesting little story. Follow me into my office where it'll be a bit warmer."

The office like the entry hall and large room was filled with photographs stretching from floor to ceiling. A moth eaten carpet, a cot, several chairs and a large fireplace filled the room. Motioning Theo and Noah to sit down near the fire the gentleman picked up a pipe, taking some time adjusting the tobacco just right. "Do you mind?"

There was something quite animated about the man, a Santa Claus clone. Noah stared in awe at the rising trail of smoke, his eyes following the white cloud drifting slowly to the wooden rafters. The short silence was broken by the sound of peat crackling "What have you learned about the McCann's from the objects you alluded to?"

"Before I answer would you know where the McCann homestead might once have been located? Yesterday Noah and I biked to the valley outside town to a spot where the road forked. Do you know that area?"

The man took a long pull on his pipe nodding.

"On Patience Lane Noah and I came to a crown in the road overlooking a large scattering of boulders, assuming they were once house foundations. Do you know the area where those rocks are located?"

Another long slow pull on the pipe yielded a knowing yes.

"One stone home was still barely standing, appearing quite dilapidated and uninhabited. Did the McCann's live near there?"

"You say you turned onto Patient Lane?"

Theo nodded saying they'd left their bikes by the side of the road and wandered into the valley of stones. "We were looking for just the right spot to have our picnic lunch."

"You said earlier you believed the last McCann left the village just after World War Two. Is that a fact you surmised from reading old letters?"

"That was what I came believe. Stories from my grandfather and father hinted there were no more McCann's in the old country and I had no reason to doubt them. You aren't suggesting McCann's still live in the area are you?"

Exhaling another large plume of smoke, the cloud engulfed the man's large face.

"I've never formally introduced myself" he said, "so let me start there so I can begin to relate a rather interesting tale."

Was the old man a bit daft Theo wondered? Lonely? A chatter box? What was putting the twinkle in his eyes?

"Will you please tell me your name," Theo asked, the request a bit too edgy.

"My name is Sander McCann, same last name as yours, born and raised in this village and as an aside I expect to be buried here in the old family plot. I'll show it to you later if you're interested. I'm seventy-seven years old and for most of those years I farmed the land until something I never anticipated happened. As they say in America fasten your seatbelt.

"It was May 17, 1941 the day I was unceremoniously evicted from my farm house and land per orders from the highest British authorities. Back then the Brits pretty much ran our country essentially making us second class citizens. That date was a few days after something quite extraordinary happened on my farm. That was nearly fifty years ago and I've never talked about that day to anyone. Why? Because I was told if I spoke about what happened I'd lose more than my home."

Thinking the man was possibly confused Theo had no idea where the story was going or how it might relate to the McCann family. Uncertain if it was the heat from the fire or something in the way the man spoke Theo began sweating.

"Tell me more about the McCann's if you don't mind. I grew up hearing my grandparent's emotional tales about the old homestead and that's what I'd like to learn about. One day I discovered a cache of old letters and faded photographs I mentioned, hidden away in an old cardboard box in out attic. When my parents passed I inherited those treasures.

"Sander, if I may call you by your first name, I'm a bit mystified. Having the same last name makes me wonder if you are connected to my relatives. I suppose it's a common Scottish name but might you be related to the McCann's living here for nearly two centuries?"

Sander closed his eyes, slowly reciting the names of his parents, grandparents and great grandparents. It took Theo only a few moments to realize he was hearing names he'd learned when pouring through the trove in the box in the attic.

19

The next words were uttered with awe. "Is it remotely possible you and I could be family? What are the chances you and I and my son Noah are related to you?"

"Well, well, well. From what you've told me I believe you would be a distant American great nephew."

Squeezing the life out of Noah's hand the words fate and coincidence struck again.

"That one building standing you saw yesterday on your exploring, well that's where I once lived as did generations of McCann's before me. That one standing home was built in the 1700's by our ancestors, although not certain if it was 1788 or 1799. I lived in that home alone beginning in 1939, a tragic year for the world because of the war. My wife Mary passed some years earlier and with her death I officially became the last of the McCann's living in Scotland. I've actually not met or talked with another McCann in nearly forty years so I'm as surprised as you probably are. I am the last and only McCann in Eaglesham."

Looking directly at Noah Sander leaned close.

"I haven't been ignoring you son, have I?" Turning to Theo when Noah didn't respond Theo began to offer an explanation. Sander rescued the moment saying the boy was certainly the shy and quiet one. Not the truth but it eased the anxiety a bit. Theo couldn't find the right words to talk about what troubled Noah and he was certain it wasn't the right time to bring up the tragic story of Noah's silence, at least not yet.

"Noah's a boy of very few words." Quickly changing the subject Theo asked if Sander was the mayor or an elected official in Eaglesham?"

"I guess you'd say I'm actually the unofficial mayor. I'm also the official town greeter, the town record keeper and part time tour guide when walking isn't hindered by my arthritis. I'm also the town crier and cursed for being the tax man. We're a very small and poor village so there's no need to hire an expensive team to manage the town's affairs. I get a meager salary which is whatever the locals collect in a hat passed around each month. I don't need much or want much so I'm okay. This area behind the great hall here I've converted into a tiny bedroom. When I lost possession of the old homestead I had no place to go but that's part of a long story."

"Why is that one home not in ruins like the others""

"It's a large part of a complicated story I'll get to eventually. That structure was the home of the McCann's for more than two hundred years until one fateful day it wasn't mine anymore. For a long time it was just me and Mary and we'd expected to live there forever. Regretfully things didn't work out the way we'd hoped and planned. If you've got some time right now and if I'm not boring your little boy, I'd like to share a very problematical tale that began more than forty years ago. I've never told another living soul what I've carried in my heart and head so bear with me because the old mind is a bit rusty. I've kept a deep and dark secret to myself expecting to take it to my grave. Your surprise appearance in Eaglesham stirred something so maybe it's the right time to let it go. Given that we're kin and I'm getting on in years it's probably time to reveal one great mystery in my life."

At that moment the front door of the town hall opened, Sander getting up and walking out into the big room. He turned back to say it was urgent town business he'd better tend to. Fifteen minutes later Sander poked his head in the office, apologizing he had some unexpected business to attend to.

"Would you and the boy like to return after dinner so we can continue talking family? It might be taking time away from your vacation so I'd certainly understand if that doesn't work."

Theo smiled saying he'd very much like to revisit. With Noah in hand they left the town hall slowly walking back to the inn. A candy shop caught Noah's eye and for having to put up with adult chatter Theo said let's buy something really sweet.

Peering into other shops was a unique experience, very different from our busy malls Theo remarked. One shop posted a welcoming sign stating

21

it had continually been doing business in Eaglesham since receiving a royal license in 1775. Noah's silence was ever present but there was light in Noah's dark eyes, a noticeable difference. He often wondered if Noah could somehow hear what he was thinking. The large bag of candy clutched in the child's hands put a little more life into his step, one of those few rewarding moments

In their room Theo drew a picture of a tree emphasizing the branches. "With this simple drawing" Theo whispered "you can make a diagram locating all your ancestors.

"I was very lucky Noah because the McCann's side of the family passed many personal belongings, stories and photographs down through the generations. Let's see where everyone belongs on our tree. Regretfully I really don't know much about your mother's side of the family but if you enjoy this exercise we can draw another tree and hopefully discover relations on mom's side of the family."

With tears welling in Noah's deep dark eyes, Theo remembered it had been a very long time since he'd mentioned Noah's mom. Noah's half smile was one of the very few ways he communicated, mostly done through drawing that spoke for him. Noah seemed rather pleased when Theo asked him to color in the leaves on the barren tree.

Rather than eating at the inn again Theo suggest they go out for fish and chips, sit by the river and watch the fisherman trying to entice large salmon to their bait. Little could Theo ever imagine he might experience even a single moment of pure peace but there it was. In short time however he would become captive to what Sander would relate.

CHAPTER FOUR

The morning was so quiet in Eaglesham the village had the feeling of a ghost town. Setting out for Sander's office in the town hall Theo had no inkling what Sander might say about the McCann family, including a secret he claimed to have kept inside for many years. Gray smoke poured from the town hall chimney, a sign of life on a very chilly morning. A warm smile greeted father and son and an offer of hot tea and something special for Noah, a McCann family recipe of hot chocolate.

The peat fire's warmth and the sounds of ancient peat crackling warmed the room and the soul. Theo wondered if Sander's tale would interest Noah so as a distraction he made sure Noah brought along a few books to read. The old man exuded charm but Theo remained a bit leery, fearing his powerful presence might intimidate Noah. Sander wasted no time declaring it was the right time in his life to relate a most unusual event. Theo asked for a few minutes to say some needed things about Noah.

With Noah not having said a word he wasn't sure where to start the cheerless tale, how to explain the devastating misfortune in their lives. With the exception of the therapists he'd taken Noah to, Sander would be the first outsider to hear the woeful tale.

Slowly and cautiously he said there'd been an auto accident seven months ago and that he and Noah had not yet recovered. "No we weren't involved in the accident but we both suffered greatly. Looking toward Noah he saw the familiar blank stare. With heavy heart he began the woeful tale about the deadly car incident.

"Noah," Theo said solemnly, "has not uttered a word since that terrible day, not a single word." Theo's s voice broke describing the arrival of the police officers and the ghastly news.

The sympathetic look on Sander's face was not missed. Rising from his chair he knelt down before Noah, taking both hands into his and smiling.

"It's okay lad. Most of us adults talk too much and really have nothing to say. I'll bet you're a good listener which by the way is a trait of the McCann clan. I'm awfully sorry about what happened and I sincerely hope you'll always remember the good things about your mum and brother."

If there was a time and moment for Noah to talk Theo prayed it was then, but it was not to be. Sander pounded his heart, then gently touched Noah's.

"Maybe it's not the right time for me to begin my long convoluted story" Sander whispered. "It pales in comparison to what you're going through so please feel free to tell me to wait for a better time.

Theo looked over at Noah, absorbed in one of his books. Please go ahead he asked.

"Before I get to the story I forgot to tell you I found a few ancient volumes in the downstairs vault that should interest you and hopefully the lad. I was terribly excited what I'd discovered and truthfully if you hadn't shown up, I probably wouldn't have seen them. The records contain nearly every detail of lives, deaths, work, education, marriage and lists of all the worldly objects left behind when the McCann's passed. The earliest documents were written more than two centuries ago, a fascinating look into our family's lives. The town records indicate how and when individual homesteads were passed down from father to son or in some cases just sold. Some of the old ledger books describe important events in the community mostly relating to harvests and changes in the town charter."

Sander handed over a box filled with pages of reproduced documents he'd spent the night organizing, Apologizing for the copies he said many of the originals were too fragile to handle. Theo guessed somewhere in those papers was the extraordinary event Sander had alluded to.

"Take all the papers back to your inn when you leave promising me you'll read every word. It'll take you a while but it's worth it. Much of the writing is difficult to decipher but you're still going to get an education. I might be able to answer any questions you have, at least I hope I can. You'll find names and dates and practically the entire history of the McCann clan, lives lived on one homestead. That was until that one fateful day which I'll get to later."

Perhaps the misfortune related to one of the Scotland famines Theo pondered. Looking again at Noah he whispered proudly that Sander was his great-great uncle. "Thanks to him you're going to be very busy soon filling in lots of names and dates on the leaves you've drawn on our family tree."

Sander apologized saying he just remembered that he had some pressing town business to attend to, saying it would be a good time for Theo to return to his room so he could bury himself in the family history. Alas the mystery would have to wait.

Awake most of the night reading the family saga did take him back to the late 1700's. The notes and ledgers were not as exciting as he'd once thought; minutia about acreage bought and sold over the years, livestock births, births and deaths of family members, income earned and taxes. It all became very tiresome reading.

The documents however brought Theo into another world and time and for that he was grateful. I'll close my eyes for five minutes he whispered to a sleepy Noah, waking up hours later in the morning discovering he was not quite halfway through the papers.

To Theo's disquiet Noah was not in his bed, nor was he in the room. Running half dressed and filled with fearful thoughts he flew down the stairs to the front desk asking Franz if he'd seen Noah. Franz pointed to a table near the fireplace where to Theo's relief, Noah and Sander

25

were eating breakfast together. Walking toward them he stopped, sensing something extraordinary was happening, not wanting to infringe on their camaraderie. Retreating back to the stairs before being seen and to their room it gave him more time to read a bit more. The vision of Noah looking so peaceful with Sander caused his mind to stray. Returning to the breakfast nook a half hour later he was greeted with laughter.

"Just two kin enjoying a delicious breakfast together," Sander said proudly.

The picture of their closeness made the entire trip worth while Theo thought.

"Did you read everything?"

Theo said he'd just finished.

"Pull up a chair, have something to eat and fire away questions, insights or thoughts."

One question begged an answer. "Tell me why you're not living in the old homestead anymore. Is the building too fragile?"

"I lived in the old homestead half my life, the building truly in poor shape but still majestic and magical. I'll start my story telling you about the frosty morning of May 11th 1941. My wife was gone and I was quite alone. All the McCann's who could emigrate to America did so just before the war so the farm was left to me to keep up and running. Determined to keep the farm operational I felt certain I'd live out my days on that wonderful plot of land but alas that was not to be. Why don't we go over to my office out of earshot of nosey Franz who by the way is the real town crier and I don't mean that in a good way."

Before settling into his tiny office in the town hall Sander posted a note on the door declaring the hall closed until noon. With an uneasy look on his face Theo had not seen before, Sander began his tale, looking subdued and serious

"Life was always difficult on the farm" said solemnly, "because the land grew harsher and more unforgiving each year. The yearly crops became little more than rocks surfacing every spring. Over grazing the land killed the soil but we didn't understand that back then. I did my best and even though the work was back breaking and frustrating, it was always done with love.

"That enchanting, peaceable homestead kept me going, a sanctuary where hard work, sweat and commitment made every day glorious. When the money stopped coming in I suspected it was time to get out but I found that impossible, being so damned proud and stubborn. 1939 was a heart rendering year in Europe and later the world. Although we were prepared for war if it came to us, no one could have foreseen the terrible destruction of farm lands and the deaths of millions. Thirty-nine was frigid and I lost most of my sheep. I prayed the land might have one or two more good years but I knew in my heart it wasn't going to happen.

"Despite devastating news from the Continent it appeared we'd be far from the war, that was until the fateful day of May 11th 1941 when something literally fell from the sky, crashing to the earth not a hundred meters from my barn."

The old man paused, looking lost in thought.

"What I'm going to relate is something I've kept entirely to myself for more than forty years. Even the people of Eaglesham don't know what I'm going to tell you. As they say in your country, an expression I like by the way, fasten your seatbelts. What fell from the sky that day changed my life and possibly the war forever."

"Please tell."

"First I have a question. Do you know the name Rudolph Hess? I ask since he's been in the news lately because of his recent death, the last remaining Nazi prisoner in the infamous Spandau Prison near Berlin."

"Sorry Sander I really haven't had time to see or read the news in some time. I do recall hearing the name though from history books."

"British authorities came to my door shortly after discovering someone fell to earth, declaring eminent domain and thusly evicting me from my home and land."

Sander lowered his head, his hands noticeably shaking.

"I've not been inside the home you viewed in that valley for more than forty years, warned of severe consequences if I ever set foot on one inch of the property. It suddenly belonged to the Crown. Because you're family I'm going to reveal what I was sworn never to disclose. You see, someone actually fell from the sky onto my farm land, arriving kind of like you totally unexpected. His name was Rudolph Hess it turned out, the number two man in the Nazi Third Reich."

After a long pause Sander whispered he needed a few moments to collect his thoughts. "The story has been buried deep inside for so long it's not easy to talk about. Bear with an old man because it feels like I'm just waking from a deep sleep, needing a few moments to steady myself."

The man was having a breakdown Theo feared, the color drained from his face and a painful look in his eyes.

"I'm suddenly not feeling particularly talkative right now so let me apologize for being unable to continue the saga right now. Why don't you both come by tomorrow morning but not here. I'd like you both to cycle out to that single standing structure you saw from the crest on Patience Lane. I'm sure you're hearing that incessant pounding at the front door telling me someone's got issues.

"Remember it's the lone structure still standing in the valley, just below the bluff where your bikes were parked. I'll need some time alone because the place has not been open for decades so don't come too early. The home where I was born has been unoccupied for years and it will certainly need quite a bit of house keeping. If you see smoke coming from the chimney don't bother knocking because the house no longer has a working front door. Just come right in."

Theo sensed the old man's angst and worry but agreed. He had no idea why Sander had been forced from the family home but it had to have been extremely dramatic he guessed. Noah seemed more animated than usual, making Theo wonder if it was something Simon said during their breakfast together. Asking if there were things he might brought along to the stone house, Sander replied not a thing.

Noah put his arms around Sander hugging mightily. It was obvious the pair bonded over breakfast.

CHAPTER FIVE

May 9, 1941

My Last Will and Testament

'My name is Rudolf Hess, born in Alexandria Egypt on April 26 1894, a citizen of Germany my fatherland. From my earliest recollections my tyrannical father smothered the life out of my childhood, making me feel I was a burden and not wanted. At the outbreak of World War One I escaped my father's influence, volunteering for the German army in 1914.

'Wounded twice I still earned my pilots wings. The day Germany surrendered was the most painful experience of my early life, more painful than being oppressed by my father. Our loss created a huge heartache, a raw numbness until the fortuitous day I met a most remarkable man.

'Rootless and aimless after the war I joined the Thule Society, a group sharing many of my sentiments and principles, most notably the fact Jews lost the war for Germany. The embarrassing surrender ended our fight for Nordic and German supremacy.

'1920 was a watershed year because I happened upon a stirring speech delivered by a man named Adolf Hitler. Overtaken immediately and uncompromisingly, I was sold on his tenets. I saw the future of a new German nation; the fledging but enticing theory of Nazism. When the speech ended I was immediately overcome by a vision to join the new party, informed I was the sixteenth person to join.

'My earliest role was that of an enforcer, something I enjoyed greatly. Speaking at public rallies Hitler was often heckled and mocked by undesirables, mostly Marxists and Jews intent on disrupting his words. I was a brawler by nature, truly enjoying using my fists to silence the demonstrators.

'Taking part in the Beer Hall Putsch our aim was to seize control of the floundering German nation. Regretfully we were defeated. My comrades and I surviving the assault by the army and were sent off to prison.

'It was my good fortune to share a cell with Herr Hitler in Landsberg Prison. His words were electric, hypnotic and so powerful they nourished me when I was starving during one of the lowest times in my life. In our cell months later I was asked to write down the great man's words and thoughts, eventually becoming the Nazi party's bible Mein Kampf.

'Herr Hitler and I and several others were released in 1925 and months later I became his personal secretary. Initially denied any official rank in the Nazi Part I was still totally enthralled with the new philosophy. In the year 1932 to my elation I was appointed Chairman of the Central Political Commission for Nazi affairs and made an SS general as a reward for my loyal services. On April 21, 1933 I was appointed deputy Fuhrer, although the position merely required me to attend ceremonial functions. My work was first-rate and a year later I was granted the title of Reich Minister, becoming a member of the Secret Cabinet Council as well as a member of the Ministerial Council for the Reich Defense.

'One of my most important duties was to introduce the Fuhrer at mass meetings. It was often said in the press I was born with a fanaticism able to drive crowds into a feverish pitch.

'I owed total loyal to the Fuhrer even though I gained the reputation of a statesman unable to understand the dynamics of power. Remaining totally and deliberately loyal to the Fuhrer I was eventually designated Herr Hitler's successor.

"Months into the War I began to conceive a secret mission, a journey I believed would save the Fatherland, my sole desire protecting the Fuhrer and the German nation. If I were successful I knew in my deepest soul that I would have fulfilled my greatest duty to Germany.

'I was involved in secret meetings exploring ways to remove Churchill as prime minister, clearing a path for negotiations for a peace treaty. Our best interest was to find someone presumably weaker than Churchill who felt war was the only answer.

'I alone understood the central tenet of Herr Hitler's geopolitical strategy, that peace with Great Britain would allow us to turn to other means to rid the world of Bolshevism. I was in tune with my Further, knowing I could execute his will without being commanded. He spoke these actual words, touching my very soul and putting ideas into my head. He declared 'I can't fly over there and beg Churchill on bended knew.' It was important to act quickly, knowing a British intermediary who might help convince England it must stand down or face extinction. I had tried to contact him alas with no response. I knew that I needed to take a more direct approach and that would come in time. Of all this I attribute to the notion I am being guided my a divine power.

'In the true event of failure however I ask that my worldly belongings be given to my Fuhrer, Adolf Hitler. Heil Hitler. Rudolf Hess.'

CHAPTER SIX

Theo became extremely restless following the stirring words from Sander, difficult falling asleep. Inundated with thoughts about what Sander might say kept him awake, wondering about the man who allegedly fell from the sky onto his farm land. The morning's dim light portended a gray day, a nasty cold chill in the air. After a warm breakfast Theo and Noah rode their bikes to the rise in the road overlooking the crumbled foundation stones. Peering down at the McCann homestead through the morning cold fog, gray smoke could be seen pouring from the chimney, a sign Sander was home once again.

Cold and windswept he and Noah were greeted by the warmth of a roaring peat fire. There were no lights and few furnishings, suggesting no electricity and certainly no running water. The burning peat gave flickering life to the dark abode. Sander called from another room saying he'd be right out with special hot chocolate for Noah and tea for Theo.

There seemed to be a glow about Sander, not sure if it was the heat from the fire or the satisfaction of being in his own home again. "Young Noah will be responsible for adding peat bricks to the blaze when needed." The words put a look of determination on Noah's face.

Sander pointed which chairs to sit in, Theo's in disrepair but still the most regal, noticeably well worn from decades of dankness and moisture. The gray mossy cold stone walls felt alive with yards and yards of spider webs highlighted by the fire light. Strong gusts of wind shook the home occasionally causing peat smoke to fill the room.

The enticing and enchanting sounds made by peat burning made the place feel not ramshackle or derelict, but actually quite quaint. Theo kept a watchful an eye on Noah, especially when he moved closer to the fire to add peat. When Sander said the fire had enough fuel the long awaited story finally began.

"Believe me the very last person occupying that very chair you're sitting on was the honorable Sir Winston Churchill, Prime Minister of Great Britain. I know that sounds crazy but I'm not an old man who's lost his mind."

It couldn't be the Winston Churchill Theo was certain. The look on Sander's face said he was deadly serious.

"The Winston Churchill," Theo asked cautiously?

The old man chuckled, winking at Noah. "There is and was only one Winston Churchill."

How did that come about Theo uttered quizzically, emphasizing the words. The dark and foreboding stone farmhouse could not have been a place for such a distinguished visitor he decided.

Leaning closer to Theo Sander's determined gaze made Theo a little leery.

"Mr. Churchill sat in that very chair on a very cold day, May 13 of 1941 to be exact. I can still hear his words in my head, insisting what was to be discussed could never leave the room.

"There was nothing calming about Churchill, a noticeable rugged edge to his voice along with a threatening posture, like a hungry dog ready to strike. In truth I was a jumble of nerves. The words I heard still live with me as if they'd been spoken only moments ago.

"Your home no longer belongs to you" he snarled. "As of this moment it becomes the official property of the British government. You have forty-eight hours to pack your belongings, never to reside here again."

The words felt like a dagger to my heart, his glare telling me there would be no debate or explanation. I reckoned it had something to do with the airman who fell to earth but I did not ask. He sat back, speaking with more civility after seeing me trembling. "It's matter of grave importance to the war effort and if my appearance here became known, our fight could certainly be compromised.

"He asked me if I'd had a visitor, a stranger in my home recently. I had not said a word up to that point so when I spoke I realized I did not recognize my own voice. Barely getting the words out he shouted speak up man, the words like an electric shock.

"What was the stranger's name he demanded. I replied he called himself Captain Alfred Horn.

Excellent was said with emphasis, a contented look on his face.

"I warn you never utter that man's name to anyone. Do you understand"? I could do little more than swallow hard and nod.

Impossible Theo thought. The real Winston Churchill would not have visited the old McCann homestead to simply evict it's tenant like a bad landlord. There was too much on Churchill's mind due to the war so could Sander have dreamed it all up?

Seeing the disbelief on Theo's face Sander continued his tale.

"Yes sir he sat in that very chair so near I could smell cigar and liquor on his breath. I know what you're thinking Theo. You're thinking I'm out of my mind, delirious and perhaps just an old fool. Well you might be right but I know what I'm talking about. You would be right to question my sanity because why in the world would Sir Winston Churchill came into a humble abode with an order of eviction? The real reason still haunts me years later."

Theo was perplexed and mystified, unable to grasp where it was all going.

"I was sworn not to discuss the Prime Minister's visitation with any living soul and I've kept my promise all these years. Every cell in my body screamed the man was deadly serious. Because you're kin and with Churchill long gone I can finally tell the real story so allow me to backtrack a bit. I want you to understand what preceded his unanticipated appearance. Two days earlier on May 10th something incredible happened here in this very place. I was tending one of the fields, counting sheep as I did everyday to see how many the wolves got. Little could I have ever known on that day everything in my world would change radically. I was twenty-five years old, living alone in this home after the clan left for America.

"May 10th I was tilling a piece of land, back breaking work I should add when I heard an unfamiliar noise from above. Not recognizing the sound I thought it could have been the wind howling. It seemed to come from the clouds so my first thought was a storm was approaching. When I scanned the skies I realized it was an airplane in a shallow twisting dive, possibly no more than several hundred feet above the farm. The sputtering engine made God-awful noises driving the sheep crazy.

"The plane made a sharp turn to the east and the motor become deathly quiet. Moments later with the nose pointing down and spiraling madly it crashed to earth in my back pasture not a hundred meters from where I stood. The plane looked like a dying bird, frightening me because I thought it might land on top of me. Beleaguered and besieged I was truly unable to move my feet. I think I might even have blacked out the moment the plane exploded into pieces on impact. There was no fire only a very pronounced hissing.

"I'd given little thought to the pilot assuming he was dead because of the hard impact. All that was left of the plane was tangled and twisted metal, believing the pilot had been killed instantly. A few tentative steps toward the wreckage felt dream like, fearing the closer I got I'd soon discover a mangled body. What if he somehow survived and needed my help I wondered? Forcing myself to inch closer to the wreckage I became aware of movement above and behind me. A billowing white parachute and the dark outline of a man attached to it took my mind off the airplane.

"My heart pounded wildly, observing the man I assumed to be the pilot falling hard, slumping to the ground, his white parachute fluttering in the breeze like sheets on a clothes line. Not far away in the pasture the sheep turned back to their grazing as if nothing happened. The pilot must be dead I whispered to the sheep. Walking nervously toward the limp body I thought I saw movement. He's alive I believed, at least for the moment.

"I shouted are you hurt but there was no response. Motioning to his harness I assumed he wanted me to free him. Entangled in metal wires and ropes I feared my effort might exasperate the injuries the pilot might have suffered. Gently removing the harness I observed the man wearing a leather flying suit.

"Clutching a canvas bag tightly to his chest the contents fell out when he tried to stand, wind blown across the field. One strong gust of wind tossed things far from the wreckage. I had not said a word other than asking if he were alright. Fluttering in the air and on the ground were British pounds, toiletries, a torch or as you say in America a flashlight, a camera, maps and charts and vials possibly filled with food or medicine. After a mutual silent standoff the man motioned me to help gather his possessions. He pointed at my home. Reaching down to help him up he pushed me away. It was then I heard his first words, a sight accent I couldn't place.

"My name is Captain Alfred Horn and I could use a sip of your legendary Scotch to gather my wits. Can you do that for me? You see I hadn't expected to run out of fuel so I was forced to bail out regretfully before I was able to reach my intended destination. It was the first time I ever parachuted and I must have blacked out."

"When I asked what his destination might be he replied the Dungavel House, the estate of the Duke of Hamilton. The estate was only twenty kilometers away I replied."

Baffled and terribly confused, Theo was having a difficult time believing the tale.

"The airman limped behind me to my home, taking a seat in this very room. With a head full of questions I couldn't get them out, remaining rather dumbstruck. He drank the scotch like a man dying of thirst.

"On the outside he appeared seemingly no worse for the fall, fortunate not to be seriously injured or killed I reckoned. When he finished his drink he asked me to walk back to the wrecked plane with him, saying something he'd brought for the Duke was possibly buried under the debris.

"I agreed to accompany him to the crash site although I really didn't want too. Reaching the debris field I had the oddest feeling we were staring down at a grave. A piece of the wreckage bore the letters ME-110 and at that moment I had the frightening feeling I was about to get involved in something sinister. Civilians in Scotland attended flight identification classes in order to identify enemy aircraft passing over the land. From those classes I knew the plane was a German Messerschmitt, beginning to understand the foreign accent.

"The man pointed toward broken fuel tanks explaining they'd been added, designed to enable him to make a nine hundred mile flight, something no one else had ever attempted. With obvious rejection his voice broke, mumbling what I believed was German. One thing was clear however. He'd come very close to landing near the residence of the Duke of Hamilton.

"It was the very first time I'd ever parachuted" he said proudly, "something I hadn't planned on. I'm an excellent and skilled pilot but I underestimated how much fuel was needed to be successful."

"Knowing what I'd heard and seen it became apparent he was a German pilot flying a German plane. The fear I felt was something I'd never experienced before. As a witness to his failure would I be shot? Slowly picking through the wreckage I sensed he was looking for something extremely important. Asking if I might help locate what he was looking for the scowl on his face was his answer. Back peddling slowly away from the site I nearly broke into a run to my home, fearing I'd be shot in the back. From a distance I watched him search, speaking in German to himself, his voice suggesting great sorrow at what appeared to be lost.

"Motioning me to come closer he asked in halting English if I knew the Duke. I replied we traveled in rather different circles, asking if he knew what that meant. He looked confused so I simply replied we lived in two different worlds. There was a look of disappointment on his face when he told me he'd once met the Duke at an air show in Germany, sharing flying stories and their experiences in various types of aircraft they'd flown.

"Captain Horn sat down among the pieces of the plane, shaking his head at the destruction of a once beautiful airplane. I said there was a telephone in the village, asking if he'd like me to call someone to let them know he was alright. His laughter frightened me.

"His next words were very unnerving, asking if I knew who he was. I said a resounding yes that he'd identified himself earlier as Captain Alfred Horn. He smiled at my response. I had a sense at that moment I was being deceived because Alfred Horn was not a German name. Shivering in the cold he asked to go back into my home to warm and think. In a softer gentler voice he apologized for the unintentional intrusion into my life, saying he wanted to share something for helping him.

"Apologizing for damaging my property he pleaded I not utter a single word about the incident to anyone. How would I explain the destroyed aircraft I wondered when someone came by? It was all so otherworldly and confusing. It wasn't every Scottish farmer who had a German aircraft crash onto their property. With a menacing scowl he said not a word at least until he met with the Duke.

"My real name is Rudolf Hess" said with an evil laugh. "Does that name mean anything to you?"

"I told him I listened to BBC news reports from time to time, some of the new stories were about Nazi leaders and what they were doing or saying. If I'd heard the name Hess I told him I didn't remember in what context."

"Keep this in mind" he said in a softer tone, "I'm not here to harm you or anyone else. I am a brother in arms with my Fuehrer Adolf Hitler, granted the great honor to be named his successor. I am a very important man so take my words seriously. Make no judgments about what you've heard about me until I've finished my work here.

"My only true desire in this life is to serve the Fuhrer as you probably would the Queen. In time the great man and I began to grow apart, especially after hearing about daunting military actions he was considering. I began to plan a secret mission in my mind, intending to visit the Duke with a plan that would accomplish two things. First, it would get me back in Herr Hitler's good graces and second, it would greatly benefit England and Germany. I was convinced a private channel for discussions with the Duke could alter the war and make us allies. When we eventually meet I want to convince him the purpose of my mission is to create a peace between Great Britain and Germany, just two old flying aces preparing the way for a justifiable peace between our two nations."

"When he told me that I began thinking I was a goner, certain to be silenced.

"I uncovered a plan generated by the highest German authorities" he added "and if put into action would entail a land invasion of the Soviet Union. Germany you may know has a peace treaty with the Soviets, each side pledging not to attack the other. The treaty however was merely a ruse created to buy time so the Fuhrer could plan war efforts against the true enemy of the Reich, the Bolsheviks. I grew extremely troubled because Germany would then have to succeed in a two front war. The Fuhrer would not have his mind changed so I devised a plan to meet with the Duke, something benefiting both England and Germany.

"I grew more and more obsessed with the idea of creating a separate peace between Germany and England. After all we are more alike than different, believing we could become respectful partners. No one knows about this private mission but soon the world will. I wish you no harm but if you don't help me make my way to the Duke's residence then you shall discover dead men tell no tales. Since I need your assistance getting to the Duke's estate, I need you alive and well so you can breath easier. The German people have no desire to wage war against a fellow Nordic nation and of that I am certain. Should I fail in my mission I believe it will truly lead to untold and needless deaths.

"Make no mistake. My mission is very risky, already coming close to costing me my life. It's imperative I convince the Duke of Hamilton if England agrees to let us have our way in Europe without English interference we can then turn our magnificent military machine against the Bolsheviks, assuring the British Empire and her colonies would be spared Germany's might.

"If I succeed it would most certainly save Britain from ultimate ruin. As I have said I have come here on a peace mission, not wanting to see a fellow Nordic nation receive the brunt of German air power. If the Duke refuses to see me or if we can't come to a mutual understanding, the German high command will certainly blockade the British Isles resulting in great starvation. The world has seen German's military might and there's no doubt in my mind it cannot be stopped.

"Why am I willingly tell you this? Because due to not having enough fuel to reach the Duke's estate I'm going to need your help to finish my mission. My original flight plan was to land close by the Duke's estate but as you saw, the plane could go no further. You will not be harmed if you escort me to the Duke's estate.

"Overwhelmed and frightened it was difficult to process that a self described high ranking Nazi unexpectedly fell from the sky onto the land of a poor Scottish farmer. Asking me to obey him I knew I should not trust him. I thought about running as far and as fast away as I could but he must have read my thoughts because he said he packed a German Luger handgun, patting his jacket as a warning. I thought once I'd lead him to the Duke's estate I would be silenced. Was the man insane or disoriented by his death-defying fall from the sky? Was his so called plan the real reason for his appearance or was he a hired assassin plotting to kill the Duke and possibly other members of the royal family? Horn or Hess never looked directly at me but when he said he needed my help, his deep black eyes put a chill in my very soul.

"I believe the Duke will be extremely welcoming and truly sympathetic to my mission," he said rather nonchalantly there might be a reward for my help.

"Was the man delusional and mad? What if I refused to accompany him to the Duke's estate I wondered? What might he do to me, knowing I was a simple farmer with little knowledge of the affairs of the world?

"I had no choice so I told him I would take him to the Duke's residence. Reaching inside his jacket my thought was he was going to pull out his pistol keeping it pointed at me until we arrived a the Duke's estate. I said I knew the forest paths well and with those words he removed his hand from his jacket bringing out a map he'd brought along.

"I must look inside the wreckage once again before we leave he said sorrowfully, because there's something I must find.

"Visiting the crash site again he became so focused I wondered if he hadn't somehow forgotten I was there. How fast or how far could I run while he dwelled on his search? Sadly my feet were glued to the earth knowing I wouldn't get far. The sound of a distant owl, an omen unnerved me even more. Picking though the wreckage he grew angrier and more sullen, shouting something about his flight plan.

"I took off in the afternoon from an airfield at Augsburg-Haunstetten he said, not sure if he was talking to me or himself.

"It sounded as if his words were an eulogy, suddenly two mourners at the funeral of his beloved airplane. This was a very special aircraft with the latest German technology and able to fly though darkness and storms he said proudly.

"I set my initial course for Bonn using familiar landmarks to orient myself. When I reached the Frisian Islands I flew in an easterly direction, flying low out of the range of British radar. Heading 335 degrees crossing the North Sea at a very low altitude I flew no higher than five thousand feet. I could finally relax my grip on the stick and slow my breathing when I approached the coast of North East England in the area of Northumberland. Praying there'd be enough light in the remaining hours of the flight I expected to find a suitable landing area. I fought to stay awake. Zigzagging for about forty minutes I saw the thickening clouds and worried they would deprive me of my prize. Flying that way I used up too much precious fuel, my auxiliary fuel tanks nearly exhausted.

"I had a certain sense which I'm never wrong about which told me I had been detected by British radar, seeing several Spitfires in the distance. It seemed apparent they were on a search mission. Failing to find me I continued to look for my intended landing site, soaring at a very low altitude over the sea. I set a direct course toward Scotland, flying so low at times I was no more than a hundred feet above the water. The only time I felt at ease was the thought my ship could easily outdistance and out fly RAF fliers. If the RAF saw me however I was certain I would be shot down.

"Looking down at certain landmarks I'd chartered I began to fret that I might not be able to find either my final destination or a safe landing site. I turned due east just off the coast of Scotland flying on fumes. Climbing to six thousand feet the engine sputtered and I realized I'd have to parachute from the plane or die. As you can see by the way I carry myself my only injury is a sore foot, unsure if that happened when I left the plane or when I fell onto the earth. The flight had not gone as well as I'd hoped but I believe in my heart it was one of the greatest achievements of my life.

"What will happen if the Duke refuses to see you I asked, immediately regretting I'd spoken. I said if the spitfires saw him they were certainly aware of his intrusion and most likely looking for him.

"Can you tell me what you're looking for in this wreckage I asked," hoping the offer to help might placate him after he'd worked himself into a snit.

"I'm trying to locate something for the Duke I brought with me, a gift for an old acquaintance. It must be here he insisted because with no fire it's got to be intact.

"I repeated I'd help him search if he would tell me what he was looking for. He didn't responds so I said I'd look about the hedge rows and thorny fields in case what he was looking for was thrown far from the plane on impact. There was no response again so I went ahead to see if I could find anything.

"Kicking around rusted tin cans and animal bones in the bramble I came to believe whatever it was had to be lost forever. Ten or fifteen minutes later looking in the direction of the wreck I observed him tuck something inside his flight jacket, a very satisfied look on his face. I was chilled to the bone by then so I suggested we return to my home and warm up. Explaining it would be a long overland trek on steep trails to reach the Duke's estate I said we should have something warm to drink."

Mercifully Sander said he wanted to brew some tea, pausing the long narration.

Several peat bricks were tossed into the fire courtesy of Noah. With Sander in the primitive kitchen Theo had time to think about the woman on the plane, his seatmate. What was her name? Oh yes, Dr. Joan Ark. Was she still in Glasgow at her conference he wondered? Would it be terribly wrong to call her at the hotel asking if she might see Noah for a few hours before going home? The thought made him feel like a cad, knowing it would be wrong asking her to work while on vacation. Besides he thought she'd probably forgotten all about he and Noah so it was all a moot point. The thought of a call for help however grew more pronounced, deciding it had to be done after he left Sander. With no phone in the old stone house Theo asked Sander if he wouldn't mind looking after Noah for an hour or so. "I'd like to bike back into town to make an important phone call."

She'd said The Glasgow Central Hotel Theo reminded himself, repeating the hotel name as if it were gold. Dialing the hotel number he asked to be connected to Dr. Joan Ark's room. Had she checked out? To his utter surprise she actually answered.

It was one of those times in his life when he was absolutely lost for the right words. Guessing she'd hang up if he didn't say something immediately he identified himself, asking if she remembered him from their flight to Glasgow a few days earlier.

"Yes I remember you but I'm curious how did you know I was staying at this hotel. Did I write it down on my business card? Noah's father, right?"

Cautioning himself not to sound desperate it took a moment to figure out what to say next. His nerves were raw until she said something quite unexpected.

"You wouldn't be calling because of your son, would you?"

She had to know Noah was troubled he sensed, his silence quite obvious.

"I realize you must be terrible busy so I apologize for calling but I have a situation I hope you might help us with." Situation he thought?

"Yes it's about my son Noah and I'm calling to ask if it were at all possible for you to see him before you leave. We're dealing with a terrible problem and even though I've tried to get help we've come up empty. I'm lost and nothing has succeeded, unable to find the right help for Noah because sadly he's not said one word since the sudden death of his mother and older brother. It's a rather long sordid tale and I don't want to waste your time so would it be possible to give me some advice over the phone. Is that okay?"

Theo's heart beat double time until she replied go ahead.

"This is what we're up against. I love my son dearly but here's the quandary. He's not said a single word in the months since we both heard about the tragic accident that broke our family apart. We've been to many professionals but none seem able to break through this terrible on going silence. I'm very confused, hurt and angry and I don't know if I can hold myself together much longer. I brought Noah to Scotland for two reasons. One to possibly connect with family because I thought it might help him discover more about himself and two, I was hoping a geographical cure could be the fixer. So far nothing.

"You mentioned your work with children to me, those experiencing traumas and your work involved treating something you called selective mutism. We both experienced a heartbreaking personal loss in our lives and although I seem somewhat capable of dealing with it, it's obvious Noah can't or won't. He simply stopped talking and I don't know how to help him so that's why this call out of the blue. If you don't have any free time would it be possible to give me the names of professionals in the States experienced with this that I might contact?"

A feeling of shame overcame Theo, of impotence and weakness. There was still time to say forget the call, sorry to be a bother.

"Okay" she responded, momentarily shaking him from some of the despair. "I can try to help but you have to understand we can't do this over a phone line. What your son needs is intense therapy which is a science so no single session or phone call can provide an instant cure. I'm staying in Glasgow two more days and after I'd planned a week by myself exploring Scotland by car and foot. I want to do some backpacking, hoping to explore the Loch Ness region. It might be possible to spend a few hours with you and Noah on my way but please understand I have no magic potion that would create a breakthrough.

"Where are you calling from and where are you staying? You're welcome to come to Glasgow but for Noah's sake he might be more comfortable in familiar surroundings. I have a rental car and I could be there in a couple of days. Please don't get your hopes too high but be hopeful. No promises because what works best is truly long term treatment. Trauma patients need time to heal but hopefully we'll make some inroads into a long twisty journey. There are several good professionals in the field of selective mutism in the States but I want you to know I've successfully treated cases and I am the best."

It felt as if the sun had suddenly appeared after a terrible storm.

"We're staying in a small village called Eaglesham, a two or three hour drive from Glasgow."

Offering heartfelt thanks Theo wondered if the doctor heard the heartbreak in his plea. There were always feelings of hope each time they were off to see a professional, only to be led down the same disappointing road with the words there's nothing we can do.

CHAPTER SEVEN

Early the next morning Noah and Theo biked back to the old homestead, greeted warmly by the intoxicating aroma of hot chocolate and real coffee. During the night Theo woke several times, Sander's curious tale on his mind. Peddling the familiar route he looked forward to hearing more of the remarkable story, if in fact Sander had all the facts correct he reminded himself. He would also let on a friend might be visiting either today or tomorrow, omitting the reason for the visit for now.

The morning was filled with more incredible stories about the airman who fell to the earth on Sander's farm. Animated at times, Sander's facial expressions and arms tossed into the air made Noah laugh. Theo wondered if his son grasped any of the story or if he was just fascinated by Sander.

There was little chance Noah would become bored with two adults caught up in conversation because an impressive collection of old toys from Sander's childhood were made available.

Sander enjoyed making Noah laugh, flapping arms like a bird accompanied by the sounds of wind blowing. Throwing himself on the floor to illustrate the pilot who fell to earth, Sander left Noah and Theo in stitches.

Later that chilly morning Noah, Theo and Sander walked to the crash site, a small depression barely visible. Anyone coming upon it could never have imagined it was caused by an airplane crash Sander remarked. Theo asked if he'd ever used a metal detector to search for parts of the plane. The response was what was a metal detector.

Staring for the longest time at the tiny hollow Theo was aware that only Sander and the late Rudolf Hess were eye witnesses to that day so long ago. Noah chased after butterflies, Sander and Theo standing solemnly as if eyeing a grave site.

"Let's return home and I'll make lunch" Sander announced. "An old fisherman friend of mine stopped by after you left yesterday with a large salmon he'd just caught. We'll get a hot fire going and I'll tell you about the British authorities who seemingly descended from nowhere into my tiny isolated world.

"I left off relating the airman and I warmed ourselves by the fire drinking hot cups of tea. He asked how long it would take to trek to the Duke's estate. Having no car I told him I wasn't certain. I'd never made the walk I explained but I knew the right pathways. I made a couple of sandwiches and filled two thermoses with tea until it was time to begin out journey. Not more than a few kilometers from my home a helicopter with no discernable markings circled over our heads, eventually landing in a nearby clearing about a hundred kilometers away.

"The rotor made the tranquil valley very noisy, brush and birds blown all about. Two uniformed soldiers jumped out running right toward us. The men grabbed the airman by his arms, pulling him toward the helicopter. I thought I'd be joining them but a third soldier exiting the craft, running toward me with a stern look on his face. He shouted above the din turn around and go home. Sporting a menacing glare he shouted not to say a word about what was taking place because I could find myself charged with treason if one word was uttered.

"The helicopter lifted off and soon all was deathly silent. The ship flew east but I had no idea it's destination."

Sander tended to the lunch in his tiny kitchen nook while Noah explored the land behind the homestead, a trusty butterfly net in hand. For a fleeting moment Noah stopped and looked in the doorway at Theo. The look on his face suggested how far could he stray from the home. The words never formed and Sander obvious to Theo's dismay said outback

49

was a fine place to search for butterflies. The long winded tale began right where he'd left off.

"Earlier I told you Sir Winston Churchill once sat in that very chair you're sitting in. I'd only seen a portrait of the great man in the town hall and would have bet the farm the prime minister of England would never stop by for a chat or a cup of tea.

"There he was in my tiny humble abode telling me his name with authority, an air of self-importance oozing from every pore in his body. I freely admit there were moments of doubt, wondering if this was the real Churchill or if I was being duped. His grand entrance, an unlit cigar clenched tightly between his teeth awed me with one thought. Could this be the real Churchill? The poor man was panting as if he'd run all the way from London, looking terribly out of shape. Recalling his portrait in the town hall I had to admit there was a very strong resemblance to the man. I still found it difficult however presupposing it might be the real deal. The man had a commanding presence I'd never seen before without uttering a word.

"His very first words ordered the soldiers accompanying him to get out of the house, keeping everyone away with no exceptions. Staring at me with the most unapproachable and imitating eyes he whispered I must listen carefully because nothing would be repeated.

"I sensed I might soon become eyewitness to something quite important, possibly about the war. He must have more pressing business than confronting a poor farmer I thought, realizing I'd been holding my breath.

"Tell me exactly what happened on your property beginning with the moment you spotted the plane to the time it crashed. Leave absolutely nothing out he warned sternly. I've received reports about the incident but you were the only eyewitness to the event. What were the airman's first words? Did he speak like an educated man? Did he have an accent? Did he appear hurt in any way? Do you think the man was rational?"

"The questions came so rapid fire I couldn't remember the first question, my nerves shot. I did my best to methodically relate the entire account, interrupted occasionally with a slight nodding of his large head. Twice I said I was just a simple country farmer with little education, doing the best I could to help the stranger. There was no response, waving his hand furiously for me to speed up.

"Alfred Horn were the flyer's first words.

"The Prime Minister demanded I speak louder, making me even edgier. Trying to remember the questions he'd asked stifled me, my mind blank believing he thought me a simple fool. Trying with great difficulty to describe all I'd seen and heard I sensed I was digging a hole for myself. If I was in trouble which I suspected, that man certainly had the power to make trouble for me.

"Sir I said with respect, "when I first saw the airman from a distance I assumed he was Royal Air Force, a victim of something terribly wrong with his aircraft. He spoke English with a slight accent which I couldn't quite place but then again, we don't get many visitors in Eaglesham. Nothing more was said for what felt like an eternity, both of us eying the wreckage. Talking more to himself than me he repeated over and over that he'd run out of fuel. Motioning me closer to the wreckage site it was then I observed something I hadn't noticed earlier. The wreckage bore German insignias. I was familiar with them because of the air raid classes we were required to take. Why would an RAF plane have German markings and insignias I wondered? Perhaps the aircraft was an RAF plane in training.

"I was too overcome to make any sense of the situation but his deep penetrating eyes pried words from me like iron filings to a magnet. Was I actually sitting two feet from the most powerful man in the British Isles, maybe the world I kept thinking? He blew smoke rings from his cigar, asking brazenly for a glass of scotch the country was noted for.

"Pouring a measured shot into a small glass the effort was met with a wry smile. I remember his exact words. So it's true all Scotsman are cheap, demanding I hand him the bottle. My hands were shaking so badly I nearly dropped it. A satisfied smile eased my anxiety a little, thanking me for my hospitality. I don't know how long we spoke although it felt like ages. Announcing he had much work to do in London he would soon take leave. The bottle was empty but the great man, if it were him seemed totally unaffected.

"When he left my home I was exhausted. Whether the pilot was Alfred Horn and the man the real Churchill, well all I could do was sit in a confused state.

"Several uniformed British solders entered when Churchill left, demanding I turn over anything the airman left behind in my home. There was one item I'd hidden away but I'll get to that later. Had I taken anything from the wreckage site I was asked. The truth was I hadn't but I never let on what the airman gave me which happened to be his personal flight jacket, a reward because I'd helped him. I was certain it had to be quite valuable so I stashed it where it could not be found. Why? I'm not really sure. The soldiers looked all about my home, taking a few things until convinced there was nothing more. When the soldiers left I found myself shivering, uncertain if it was the dying fire or the fear and confusion I felt.

"That was the last of the soldiers except for one lone rifleman who'd pitched a tent nearly on top of the crash site. One thing was certain because there was a loud rumbling in my gut. Had I gotten myself involved in something boding great danger?

"When I heard the sound of the last helicopter taking off the house shook, fearing it would collapse on top of me. Time passed but I couldn't guess how much until I noticed the drained bottle of scotch whiskey near the fireplace. I know some of the local drunks in the village but not one of them could have matched what that man imbibed. Ordered to remain indoors for two hours I was told if I obeyed then I might be allowed to continue my chores.

"I must have fallen asleep mulling over the events of the day because when I awoke it was dark outside. Several hundred yards from my home seeing a small campfire, I eyed the lone soldier's tent, a reality check telling me it wasn't a dream. I crept slowly toward the area where the plane fell to see what might have been left behind. To no surprise there were no signs of the crash, as if nothing ever fell to earth, only a slight impression barely visible in the moonlight. Oddly it felt as if I were standing before a new grave in the village cemetery.

"I got a roaring fire going, ruing the reality my life would never be the same again. I'd aged years in a matter of hours, caught in something I could not talk about nor even explain to myself. Putting the events of the day out of my mind was impossible, but mercifully the sounds of peat crackling in the fire allowed the first brief peaceful moment of the day.

"I stayed by the fire during the night nodding off only to wake with a start minutes later. During those awful moments I found myself thinking why me, feeling terribly sorry for myself. I got up to make sure the flight jacket was still hidden and not found by the soldiers. Curiously the empty bottle of scotch was gone, as was the glass. Searching for an ashtray containing his cigar ashes well, that too was gone. I could only guess the lone remaining soldier came into my house during the night to remove all evidence of Churchill's visit. Even though I was ordered to have no contact with him I tiptoed to his camp site half in anger and half out of curiosity. Hesitating for a few moments I told myself it was not the right time but I couldn't turn back because I desperately needed answers.

"Trying to remain calm was impossible, paranoia gripping my entire body. Turning back toward my home a sudden shot of audacity struck me.

"Could it have been someone other than Churchill in my home was the first question I wanted to ask, although I suspected a simple foot soldier wouldn't know that. Not to get too far ahead of myself I will tell you this. Days later I found a three day old edition of the morning Glasgow paper left in the town hall entrance way. On the front page was a picture of Sir Winston Churchill giving a speech to the Moroccan parliament, asking for their support in the war effort against the Axis powers.

"That story made me certain I'd lost my sanity. Usually not up to date with worldly news, I'd become obsessed with what Churchill was up to. The date on the byline grabbed me as if I'd picked up a live wire. According to the article the speech was delivered on May 13, two days after the airman fell from the sky, the day Winston Churchill allegedly appeared here. How could he be in Morocco and my place at the same time? Fearing I was losing what was left of my fragile mind I'd have given anything to have a snort but thanks to Churchill, the liquor cabinet was empty. It was a full week before I was able to sleep more than an hour without waking with frightening dreams in my head. If the soldier would not or could not help me I knew there were other uniformed men on the mission and perhaps I could seek them out. As to when and how the remains of the crash were removed, it had to be during the two hours I was told to stay indoors. Staring at the tent pitched over the crash site I was smacked in the face by the reality there no longer was a crash site, no broken pieces of airplane, nothing.

Chapter Eight

"If it wasn't for the lone soldier, a captain I later learned who was left behind to watch over me and my home I never would have learned a few truths, definitely things not meant for my ears. Remember this was a long time ago and until your unexpected arrival there was no one I could tell this too. The townspeople would think I'd gone daft if I'd explained all I'd seen and heard.

"Hoping the soldier might be sympathetic to what I'd been through, I made a calculated decision to bring him a canteen of hot tea with fresh scones, hopefully to learn things that were tearing me apart.

"My back pocket contained a flask filled with a hidden cache of home brew I'd found, hopefully to loosen his tongue. Having no idea his rank I assumed it was rather low due to his duty, so perhaps he truly knew nothing. I stared at that tent, illuminated by a near full moon and his small camp fire. I tied to convince myself I was about to place myself in a precarious situation. Oh hell I thought. I truly had nothing to lose.

"It was terribly cold and in truth I felt a bit sorry for the poor lad, loading my fireplace with extra peat to make it more enticing, hoping the earthy smelling smoke might stir the soldier. Careful not to sneak up and possibly get shot, I walked heavily, praying I wasn't putting myself in harms way. Assuming he was armed I proceeded with much caution.

"When I was no more than ten feet from his tent I thought of the right words, asking if he'd like a mug of hot tea perhaps with a dash of home brew to take the edge off the cold. When there was no response I turned away, retreating toward my home. A moment or two later I heard his voice.

"I'm on duty and unable to imbibe any alcohol but hot tea would be very welcomed. Reaching his hand out of the tent I placed the mug in his hand then began the slow retreat to my home. I thought that was as far as things would go but I was wrong. I'd gotten no more than a few feet when he called out.

"If you wouldn't mind I'd like to take up your offer and add a little zest to the tea, that is if your offer still stands. Well sir, one shot led to another and then the magic words. He said he wouldn't mind a little company because he was quite cold and lonely. I told him he was more than welcome to come to my home, enticing him with the words I have a very warming peat fire going. There was no response but a few seconds later the tent was unzipped, followed by footsteps.

"Settling in close to my fire as we're doing right now I observed smoke rising from his damp clothing. This could get me court-martialed he slurred, saying I was never to tell another soul about our meeting. A few shots later he was obviously tipsy and curiously I began to feel a bit ashamed. If I promised not to repeat anything he might tell me, he'd explain why British authorities were so interested in the farm and the airman.

"By then the drink had gone straight to his head but instead of joy I felt even more guilty, ruing the thought I might be getting the poor boy into big trouble. Guessing his age somewhere in his mid to late thirties part of me said end the rendezvous, saving us both from potential problems. What I'm going to tell you was slurred, told I would have to take the words to his grave. One last shot of my home brew emboldened him more."

Looking over at Noah reading his Loch Ness book, Theo was pleased the boy wasn't paying any attention to the adults. The peaceful look on Noah's face spoke volumes.

"Keep in mind this happened more than forty years ago so my wits and memory aren't as sharp as they once were. High on the homemade brew the soldier began talking, actually more like rambling.

"Have you ever heard the name Rudolf Hess he asked and if you have, what do you know about him?"

"At the time I really didn't know anything so I begged him to tell me. If you read articles in you local paper or have seen newsreels at your local theater he stammered, you'd have seen and heard the words of a very high ranking member of the German Nazi party.

"Everyone knows the name Adolf Hitler but Hess? The man was once deputy to the Fuhrer he said, the successor if anything happened to Hitler. I learned much about Hess in our unit's all-night strategy session preparing for this mission. I'll share some of that with you but you can't tell a soul. I knew little to nothing about Rudolf Hess but I got an education that evening, a session lasting into the early hours of the morning. Hess was the Minister of the Reich Defense we learned.

"I'll give you a little history lesson. In the late thirties the fledging Nazi Party attempted to take the reins of the German government by force. That's a well known fact, a sad and failed chapter in German history. When Germany invaded Poland in the late 30's Hess had been privy to all of Hitler's war plans. The unit that descended upon your farm was assembled rather quickly when British intelligence learned of Hess' capture here. Rumors were he'd fallen out of favor with Hitler, shunned aside by others in the party and possibly vulnerable so a valuable catch. The plan was to make sure we got hold of him and held him in seclusion before others knew he was here..

"His motive for the flight became a common theme on the BBC. The world was told Hess in an effort to gain Hitler's confidence back went rogue. My unit was briefed by British intelligence so we knew it was going to be something really important. We were instructed that our mission was to recover everything related to Rudolph Hess including his crashed airplane. Whatever we found we were ordered to turn over to our superiors without comment or delay. We were dealing with a very delicate situation we were told and not to contaminate any possible evidence. The airman was not Albert Horn as you were told, but the indomitable Rudolf Hess.

"He was a very skilled pilot using his flying skills to undertake a very difficult journey. Why risk his life? Something for future historians to ponder I guess.

"History books one day might explain that on May 11th he took off from a German airbase we'd been monitoring. Intelligence suggested his destination was somewhere in the British Isles. Allegedly he left behind several handwritten notes alluding to a peace mission but we were not given any details.

"British intelligence learned weeks earlier Hitler's Machiavellian plan was to tear up the peace agreement with the Soviet Union and attack. Hess supposedly fretted about the planned surprise attack along the Soviet Union's western border. The Brits intercepted several telegrams regarding Germany's war plans. A two front war would be the end of Germany Hess and others feared, but obviously not Hitler.

"Hess as it turned out once met briefly with the Duke of Hamilton during the Berlin Olympics in 1936. Half of the soldiers in my unit were dispatched to his estate to protect him. Hess according to rumor claimed to have found an Englishman who could be trusted. His final destination was unknown until RAF units got him under surveillance.

"My unit was ready to go on a moment's notice once Hess' destination was discovered. It turned out to be this plot of land. His preference was the private airstrip belonging to the Duke and if Hess had gotten there before us, there was a good possibility we might not have found him. By the way the Duke was briefed about Hess's expected arrival.

"From what I learned Hess flew in a Messerschmitt ME110, an aircraft the RAF tracked.

"My team was the first to deploy by helicopter onto your farm, team two to the Dukes residence and team three into the immediate area making certain others were not involved. When we heard the definitive report that his plane crashed we were initially told the German pilot died in the wreckage. Obviously that turned out to be false. Once on the ground we were ordered to find and collect all evidence near the plane crash site.

"How was British intelligence able to infiltrate Hess world? We weren't privy to that but were told if we couldn't locate him, the course of the war could change dramatically. A leather pouch was found containing papers but per orders they were turned over to the commanding officer unopened. What might have been inside the pouch is only known by a few so it's significance is anyone's guess. Rumors were rife the Germans were preparing a blockade of the British Isles so the question on everyone's lips was, was Hess here to evaluate our defenses?

"The officer thanked me for the hot tea and spirits and the chance to warm his frozen bones. The more he spoke the sorrier I felt for the poor soldier, learning some time later the explanation was the real deal.

"Until the soldier and I spoke I was still fairly convinced it actually was Captain Alfred Horn on a mission to visit the Duke.

"Asking the captain if he would like to spend the night by the fire he replied no. There were a few more hours before sunrise and when he retreated toward his tent he paused, asking me to walk with him afraid he'd get lost. I walked and he stumbled to the tent site using flashlights. Everything found around the wreckage by that time was in the hands of British intelligence. As an aside what was found is a very closely guarded secret to this day. Why would a commissioned officer be assigned that remote duty? He replied he was the only one in the unit who spoke perfect German.

"We went our separate ways, his words about Hess etched in my mind. How could I explain the curious series of events when nothing was certain or made sense. The only certainty was the reality my life had been unexpectedly thrown into what historians would later agree was one of the greatest mysteries of the war.

"My old life was over, the new one in turmoil. The work on the farm and the town hall was put aside because of a terrible bout of mental paralysis. Ten days after the man landed on my farm a package arrived at my office and inside was a letter addressed to me. I still have it tucked away someplace.

"It was an unconditional demand to leave my home, the deed for the property officially belonging to the Crown. That was the beginning of my long exile from the family homestead until you arrived.

"Troubled by where I might live, I considered moving into a friends home for a few days until I found a new place. Fearing I could easily disrupt his household with my life in panic I decided not.

"Walking back to the homestead a week or so later I saw signs declaring trespassers would be prosecuted to the fullest extend of English law. A few nosey but kindhearted townspeople bombed me with questions about what was happening. Even if I could reply I simply could not explain."

Greatly troubled and disillusioned by Sander's lurid tale Theo searched for the right words to say how sorry he was for the intrusion into a serene pastoral life. How was it possible the war thousands of miles away could create such great chaos in the life of one poor farmer in a small village in Scotland?

It was getting late and time to cycle back into town with Noah before darkness. Sander looked worn out, reliving the incident must have felt like running a marathon Theo suspected. Stay the night there he wondered to make sure he was okay? Sander was obviously a very proud independent man, guessing the answer would certainly be no. The plan was to return late morning the next day. Never far from Theo's thoughts while Sander spun his tale was Dr. Joan's visit. Could she somehow help poor Noah?

At the inn Noah was absorbed in a book about the Lock Ness Monster, a gift from Franz the innkeeper. Writing notes from time to time one deeply touched his heart. 'Could we travel and search for the monster one day?' We might just do that was the reply. Homemade Ice cream delivered by

Greta to the room and a few extra peat logs tossed into the fireplace were truly welcomed.

A bit after sun up Franz knocked on the door whispering there was a phone call for Mr. Theo McCann. Noah was sound asleep so he tiptoed down the stairs thinking it could only be one person. To his great surprise and joy it was that person. Dr. Joan asked for directions to the inn and would it be possible to book a room for one night?

She was actually coming he nearly shouted out, shortly after awash in a tidal wave of guilt. Selfish he said aloud, startling Greta. Hell of a way to start a new day he said to Franz who had no idea what Theo was talking about.

Gray smoke poured from the homestead's chimney, a welcoming sight because the bike ride was on another cold misty blustery morning. Theo's mind flip flopped between Noah and Dr. Ark and Sander's hypnotic tale. There was also a bit of unfinished business, hoping Sander could help fill in the branches on the McCann family tree with names and maybe dates.

Noah got a warm bear hug and a mug of his beloved hot chocolate. To his obvious delight on his special chair near the fireplace was a collection of children's books about Scotland, courtesy of the traveling librarian. As usual the peat fire became hypnotic. Noah handed Sander the crude family tree drawing, Sander slapping his knee shouting good job lad. "We'll begin to fill it in later this morning."

The ongoing saga about the airman who fell from the sky picked up where Sander left off. Distracting was the wonderful aroma coming from the kitchen. Sander said there was a very special delicacy in the oven, something called haggis.

"I know all this talk about Hess can be drawn out and boring" he shouted from the kitchen. "I know you didn't come to Scotland to listen to an old windbag talk about ancient history. That said you're doing an old man a special favor letting me free up things I've bottled up ever since that fateful day in May of 1940. As I said yesterday I truly had no idea I was sharing bread with a top Nazi official. You know what I think about most? What was so valuable in that pouch. Why am I curious about that? Because of the forlorn look on the airman's face when it became obvious that he could not locate what he was looking for. The British army team searched every square inch of the farm even miles from my place. What they were looking for had to be extremely valuable."

Engrossed once again in Sander's tale, Theo realized he was spending hours talking to Sander which meant taking valuable time away from Noah.

"Hess' abnormal journey" Sander emphasized," turned out to be one of the most bizarre episodes of World War II. A one man peace mission? Undertaken because he feared a German invasion of the Soviet Union would mean a two front war and likely the end of the Third Reich?"

Theo found it difficult to concentrate, thinking about Dr. Joan Ark and if some good would come from her gracious visit. His time with Sander would be less at least for a day but he figured he'd understand. What if she arrives at the inn early and he was not there he fretted? It would be a thankless slap in the face.

Not sure when he'd return to the homestead hearing the rest of the Hess saga, Theo gave something for Sander to ponder. "Would it be alright to bring along a lady friend tomorrow?"

"No sense spending good money when you and Noah and your friend can stay here with me. You know us Scotsmen. We're pretty frugal and I'm sure Noah and your friend would enjoy exploring the acres of trails, caves and ancient Roman ruins while you and I finish up this Hess business. Does that sound like a good plan?"

Theo said it did but he didn't want to impose on his uncle, explaining he'd already paid for the rooms.

Theo needed to get back to the inn to await Dr. Joan's arrival so he told Noah to gather up his things. From the look on Sander's face Theo was certain the wily old man suspected there was more to just a visit, winking making Theo blush. Could he and Noah pick up supplies at the market Theo asked? With a wry smile he replied thank you no. You just enjoy your time with the lady,

CHAPTER NINE

Franz handed Theo a note the minute he walked in. 'I told the front desk I was going out to take in the sights about town. By the way this place is enchanting.'

Getting comfortable on the old sofa nearest the fire felt especially warming with Noah by his side, waiting for a saint on a chilly afternoon. Keeping one eye on the front door he nearly forgot what Dr. Joan looked like. How to seem and act normal and not sound desperate or panicked might be impossible he feared. He hadn't told Noah about the visit but did say a lady friend was coming to visit them.

Did the boy remember the kindly lady who'd given up her seat on the plane so he could have the window he wondered? Noah seemed blasé, reading about castles of Scotland.

"Noah our friend is walking around the village but she'll be back soon because she's staying here. I'd very much like you and I to spend some time with her because she's a very smart lady. I don't believe you heard us chatting on the plane because you'd fallen right to sleep so you probably don't remember much about her."

There was no reaction, the boy more interested in the book and the pop up 3D castles.

"Her name is Joan Ark and she's a doctor helping people with problems. If you don't want to spend time with her that's okay but she could help us with what we've been through. Would you mind spending a little time with her before we return to Sander's place this evening? Noah seemed to think about it, Theo reemphasizing she was a very smart woman. Remember the doctor's I took you to when we were home?"

Noah winced, an appropriate response Theo noted.

"Dr. Joan is a kinder doctor so don't worry. No shots and I'll be by your side all the time. There's a good chance she might want to spend time talking with you alone and I think that's good. The best part? I think she knows all about the Loch Ness Monster and Scottish castles."

As expected there was no expression on Noah's face and sadly, no verbal response. He did manage a nod, one of the few acknowledgments shown at times.

Greta brought a plate of cookies over just out of the oven presenting them to Noah. What a gracious lady Theo thought. No sign of the doctor yet.

The warmth and crackling sounds made Theo sleepy, Noah dropping his book, his eyes closed resting against his father's side. Hoping for a miracle he'd learned the hard way not to set his hopes too high. There were too many letdowns. Trying not to set himself up for another failed mission he didn't believe he could handle one more disappointment. Questions flooded his mind, the most frightening would Noah ever speak again.

Hearing the old oaken front door opening he was suddenly dumb struck. Shaking the sleep from his tired head there she was, making his heart beat wildly. After offering a heartfelt apology for not being at the inn when she checked in, what followed was a feeling of amazement she was really there. Noah remained sound asleep, Dr. Joan saying don't wake the boy.

With time limited he wondered if he should jump right into the gory details about the great tragedy in their lives. Trying to find the right words were difficult so instead he thanked her for giving up precious days of her vacation.

How'd your presentation go he asked, and should he wake Noah? Dr. Ark smiled at the boy, shaking her head no. Any trouble finding the place? Unable to slow down he knew he was losing control, too obviously not thinking or acting logically. What was her first impression of the town he asked? Without waiting for an answer he fired more questions. She smiled, telling him to relax and enjoy the moment, then asking why he and Noah came to Eaglesham. .

"I desperately needed a quiet vacation and with our lives deteriorating daily sometimes hourly, I thought getting far away from our terrible situation might be curative. The reason for Scotland and this particular village is because my ancestors settled here centuries earlier before migrating to America. I thought touching the lives of Noah's ancestors might jar something loose and make him talk again."

Tell me a bit about your ancestors, she asked.

"Well I wasn't born here but my grandparents and parents were, settling in upstate New York where I was born. My grandparents and parents eventually passed and I adapted to the reality that I was without family. I have no brothers or sisters, only a lone Scottish clan in the old world, my only true foundation. That pretty much sums up why we're here. My wife and I had two sons but if you don't mind I'd like to save that for another time when I tell you more about why we're here.

"Our first full day we began looking into the McCann family history and out of the blue, something quite remarkable happened. To my amazement I discovered a grand uncle was alive and well and living here, the last of the Scottish McCann's. My initial plan was to attempt to locate old town records that might enlighten me as to where our ancestors once lived and worked and where they might be buried. It was really beyond belief discovering a relative actually still resided here."

So far so good Theo thought, wondering if she could sense the apprehension and edginess. Not wanting to get into Sander's life or his Hess fascination, he said it was good discovering kin.

"We've only been here a short while but after connecting with this man he soon began relating a most remarkable story. The abridged edition is that something quite extraordinary happened on his property some forty years ago, casting a long shadow that still lingers. A stranger arrived rather unexpectedly at his farm, that being back in May of 1941. I spent hours listening to his tale about a person who literally fell to earth onto his property. The man was parachuting from a stricken airplane and of all the places to land it happened to be on Sander's farm. I shouldn't be running off at the mouth like this but I wanted you to know the stranger was none other than a very high ranking Nazi official named Rudolf Hess. There's a lot more to the story which is easier to talk about than explaining the struggles Noah and I are experiencing. Forgive me for rambling."

Dr. Ark nodded toward Noah who was waking.

"Hi" she said. I'm Joan Ark or if you'd prefer you may call me Dr. Joan. Saint Joan Ark is how my name appears on my birth certificate but I think you probably don't know anything about my namesake. I'll tell you why it's a very special name when we get to know each other.

"I sat next to you on the airplane several days ago but you fell right to sleep so you probably don't remember me. I do remember you though. Your father said you were very smart and inquisitive, meaning you like to figure out how things work. I told your dad my specialty is working with children who've experienced something unpleasant in their life. Do you know what the word trauma means?"

There was no response.

Theo's stomach was in knots, Noah's silence like punches in the gut. He started to answer for Noah but before he said two words Dr. Joan shook her head no. He immediately realized she did not want the father to speak for the child.

"Your time is so valuable so is this a good time to tell you everything?"

Dr. Joan shook her head and said not just yet. Addressing Noah again she asked "would it be alright if I have dinner with you tonight so we can get to know each other? I don't know about you but I'm starved."

Theo thought of the phrase, do you believe in miracles?

Agreeing to meet in the dining room in an hour Theo said it had been a very long day for Noah and it might be better if he got some needed sleep, allowing the adults to talk. Dr. Joan said if that was what Theo preferred it was fine with her.

Running a warm bath then tucking Noah into the big comfortable feather bed, the evening's bedtime story began. Keeping an eye on the time he began to think of his meeting as a rendezvous with destiny.

With Noah sleeping soundly it was finally time to tiptoe out of their room. Descending the stairs he hoped there wouldn't be a dining room full of townspeople or guests. He was relieved to see no one. She had to know Noah was not shy nor was he deaf he reminded himself. Reliving that haunting visit by the police would not be easy but some of the trepidation lessened when he saw her sitting by the fire.

Greta came by to tell them what she was preparing in the kitchen and then left the two alone. Theo felt the dam holding back his life breaking.

"The professionals we sought in the States listened but offered little hope Noah could be helped. Every doctor came highly recommended, each appointment approached with anticipation and the wish Noah could be helped. The exploratory hour sessions eventually dissolved into disappointment and for me, a great sorrow I could not show. I blamed myself because I'd waited too long to get Noah into therapy. I'd hoped for a dramatic and sudden cure at any given moment but that never happened. Driving home in silence after those intense hours I found myself gripping the steering wheel so hard I thought it might break. I often had to remind myself to avoid the intersection where the accident took place."

Theo felt so tightly wound he feared he'd unravel, becoming a sobbing mess. Rehearsing what he'd plan to say to Dr. Joan was for naught because everything had become jumbled in his head. Would Dr. Joan herald some kind of breakthrough or was there going to be another heartfelt disappointment? He excused himself to check on Noah and to toss an extra peat log into the fire. Standing over the sleeping boy he felt nothing but great sadness.

Ordering wine turned out to be a mistake. Theo could not bring the chalice to his lips for fear his trembling hands would spill red wine all over himself. Talking about the quaintness of the village was easier than explaining he felt as if he were drowning.

Chatting about their travels and lives, the benign conversation and the warm fire evaporated bits of apprehension and awkwardness. Theo talked about the short stories and novels he'd had published and his junior college history teaching. Two noble ways to live Dr. Joan replied.

"Tell me about the work you do Dr. Joan."

"I work with traumatized children at a private institute in Connecticut."

There was no question in Theo's mind after Dr. Joan begin describing her work and reciting her background that she was exceptionally knowledgeable, hoping she truly was a saint. She claimed she needed more hours each day to do her work, traveling quite often to children's institutes around the nation and globe. She admitted she was on everyone's wish list to lecture and teach. Theo was absorbed, grasping the technological ground breaking work she did with children at her institute.

If there was a time to introduce Noah it was show time.

"Dr. Joan, Noah's Teachers, school psychologist and pediatricians said they understood what happened to Noah but why he wasn't responding was difficult to explain. Before I go on though would you tell me why someone as important as you agreed to take time out of your free days to see me and Noah?"

Dr. Joan's face lit up.

"I decided to take you up on your invitation for two reasons. One, I recognized certain behaviors and was pretty certain your son was experiencing difficult times. To a therapist it was quite noticeable, not quite like a flashing neon light but the subtle I'm confused and terribly lost aura. I treat many children like Noah, many silent and unable to cope with issues preceding their change in behavior. I noticed a certain look about Noah and it touched me deeply, knowing it was not a case of shyness or tiredness. I'm attracted to struggling souls like Noah and I hope I never lose that feeling. Two, I heard an urgent sense of loss and sadness in your voice when we talked on the plane and then again when we talked on the phone. If a life guard off duty observed someone drowning in a lake is there an obligation to help? I didn't want to talk about Noah during the flight because it was not the right time or place, nor did I want to turn our flight into a therapy session without being asked. I was very surprised I'll admit when you called.

"This might be the time for you to tell me what's going on with Noah. Hopefully we can scratch the surface a little and possibly continue some therapy later in the States. I'm a very good listener but I can only help when someone is honest and open. I'm not a mind reader but I've been trained to identify even the least obvious distress in children, their eyes having a way of speaking. Don't feel threatened by what I might say or what I might ask. Some parents don't let me do my job I admit I'm good at and that makes the work more difficult than it should. Let's start by you telling me what life was like for you and Noah before he stopped speaking. Was Noah a normal young boy?"

The words were food to a starving soul. Describing the horror at the dreaded intersection wasn't easy but the more he spoke the more the tamped down feelings surfaced. He referred to the event as a nightmare, the words not sounding like his own voice but the voice of a stranger. Deep wounds surfaced like air bubbles in water.

"The moment the door opened and seeing the two police officers I knew right away they'd brought bad news. My wife should have been home hours earlier and I was already quite worried. I'd heard sirens blaring for nearly twenty minutes and somehow I knew why. I can still recite word for word what the officers said."

"What was your first reaction to those painful words?"

"I haven't told anyone this before but I had an overwhelming feeling of guilt because I was not with them. I failed to protect my family so what kind of husband and father was I?

"I was overcome with a kind of pain I'd never experienced. Thinking back I probably just saw the officer's lips moving after their initial words. Noah was by my side, looking in awe at the police. He's a very curious child but it was obvious there was no visible reaction."

"The days after are mostly a blur and I think I sleep walked and stumbled through life. I don't remember the exact moment when I realized my child hadn't said a single word, too distracted and distraught to notice early on. The hours and days passed in a fog making me believe I'd lost two sons and not one.

"Noah started sleeping in my bed each night. I'd lay awake checking to make certain he was breathing, taking solace in his pure innocence. I was overwrought when I saw the way he'd use his left leg to push aside his blanket, just like his mother. Days passed with Noah not saying a word, as if he were wearing a mask, as still as a statue. My emotions ran the gamut from grief and anger and disappointment to fear and frustration.

"There were moments those first weeks when fury hit so hard and unexpectedly I became alarmed I'd harm myself or worse. The silence tortured me. I saw the face of my innocent child blank, wondering if he'd simply shut down forever. I prayed for a magic prescription or a cure that might make the horrors go away or at best become manageable, but nothing in our daily lives suggested time would heal our wounds. One of the therapists declared Noah had built an impenetrable wall around him and nothing was getting in or out."

"I'm going to need you permission to work with Noah" Dr. Joan replied, "so there are things I need you to understand. Noah is going to need long term therapy and in my short time here as I said we'd be fortunate to scratch the surface. If I'm able to begin defusing the ticking time bomb in you both and allow some of the built up pressure to escape we'd be doing well.

"You've both experienced something terribly horrific and I'm sure that you understand you're both headed down a very steep dark abyss. I'd like to spend time with you alone after I see Noah because you can't help him the way you feel right now. I know it's terribly painful recreating the events of those heartbreaking days but mourning and talking about it is healthy. Psychological wounds are more difficult to heal than most other medical afflictions and this one is huge. Of course if you'll allow it and Noah agrees I'd like to see him alone.

"My thoughts from what you've told me so far and what I've observed is that we're looking at a post traumatic stress disorder right in the face. It's what soldiers experience in war even if they're not physically wounded and the longer it festers the more difficult it becomes to treat. You're both experiencing survivor's guilt feelings and that goes hand in hand with the inner rage you described. Children are better able to recover from trauma than adults but patience is required. I'll gladly pass up some of the time I'd planned for trekking in Scotland to work with you. Usually at this point I discuss my rather steep fees but in this case, please know that will not be an issue. Tell me more before I see Noah."

CHAPTER TEN

"Noah's been unable to verbalize ever since the nightmare that broke our family apart. It's as if he's stopped living when he should be developing so many critical skills."

"Very true because Noah's brain is still developing normal thoughts and actions. As I've said children are more resilient than adults so don't try to put yourself into Noah's shoes. Don't force him to talk because I guarantee it won't help. Having deep intense therapy usually provides an opportunity to lead a normal life again. There's no magical elixir so given what you and Noah have experienced, think long term and not a quick fix.

"Consider this. In the event of trouble on an airplane parents are directed to put their masks on first before their children. There's a reason for that.

"Listen to your heart and not the words churning inside confusing and taunting you. Be compassionate in all that you do and say although I'm sure you are. Try not to let him perceive anger or distress on your face if possible. Children read their parents very well and at his age he senses your emotions without you saying a word.

"Write down the names of the professionals you sought for me and any advice offered. Children very rarely recover on their own but believe it or not they can with the right treatment. You're Noah's safety net and what he's telling you by not taking is that he feels helpless. He'll always look to you so your demeanor can offer stability and hopefully stop the downward spiral. Children do know when their parents are faking life. We don't know what's going on inside in many cases but a good therapy team like scientists peering under a microscope will get to the smallest details. Think tenderness, as if you might be handling a piece of fragile glass. Like you Noah feels guilty because he wasn't there to protect his mother and older brother. I caution you there's no timetable for healing and that can be frustrating. Some children recover slowly, others quickly but most do in time. You're carrying very heavy loads and you'll both need much strength to bear them. On the plus side Noah's at an ideal age for help and support. The typical treatment plan is first to reduce the stress symptoms, then provide coping skills. Noah is not the only eleven year old to lose a parent. When you return home go about your usual routines because a predictable home life will make Noah feel safer. Down the road he should be able to better understand that the accident was not his fault. Don't force him to talk about that terrible day until he lets you know he's ready. You'll know when that day arrives.

"Again with your permission I'd like to spend time alone with Noah. Do whatever you've planned for the day tomorrow and let Noah know that I'm just tagging along. Remind him we met on the plane and tell him I too love to explore new places and am fascinated by the Loch Ness Monster. I saw him reading a story about Nessie earlier and that might be a good starting point. At the end of my day with Noah I'll give you an honest assessment and we'll see where we go from there to rescue him.

CHAPTER ELEVEN

Theo lay next to Noah on the bed all night feeling calmer because of the hours spent with Dr. Joan. The next day's plan was to revisit Sander, bringing friend Dr. Joan along.

That night Theo dreamed about the circus and tightrope walkers performing without nets, jugglers tossing emotions rather than bowling pins and escaped lions.

The morning was warm for a change and all sunshine, the cold fog gone portending a good outdoor day for Noah. Finishing up breakfast Dr. Joan strolled into the tiny breakfast nook saying she'd drive everyone to Sander's when ready.

Driving the now familiar road allowed Theo a little time to give Dr. Joan a crash course, an abbreviated version of the dramatic events that happened in Sander's life.

As usual Sander's first order of business was giving Noah a big bear hug, asking if he'd like to borrow a special butterfly net to explore around the homestead. To my amusement Dr. Joan said she loved butterflies, asking if she might come along. Theo realized he hadn't done a proper introduction, a disapproving look from Noah prompting him. Retrieving the net Noah took Dr. Joan's hand and lead her outdoors. Holding back a heartfelt surge of emotion, Theo watched the pair run about after butterflies, Noah leading the charge laughing.

When they were out of sight he offered Sanford an explanation and the real reason for Dr. Joan's appearance. From the devious look on Sander's face Theo suspected his uncle detected some romantic interest, the furthest thing from reality.

A few extra bricks of peat tossed in the fireplace meant settling in for a spell. Sander asked what he'd said about the airman to Dr. Joan. A short version was the reply.

After the previous night's meeting with Dr. Joan Theo felt more sure of himself, ready if necessary to talk about the accident. Sander was a great talker and as Theo discovered even a better listener, the tragic tale a bit less threatening. It felt good to talk talking about that day surprising him, something he could not imagine happening. Sander's response was touching his heart, then reaching across and touching Theo's saying God Bless you and Noah.

As usual Sander was in a talkative mood, saying he'd like to share some things he'd learned about the airman over the years.

"Getting information about Rudolf Hess is and was not an easy task, especially for someone living so remotely. For good or bad Eaglesham is a village where everyone knows your business so some things are best kept to oneself. I've kept this entire Hess saga to myself for more than half my life and like you am finally able to talk about difficult things. We're not hicks or as backward as many city people would believe here. The books I get hold of were delivered by the traveling librarian who comes to the village once or twice a month in her large van. She'd always ask what she could pick up and drop off on her next visit. I was always dutifully prepared with a list I'd spent time organizing. I read many history books about Nazis, the most barbaric people the world had ever known, dutifully jotting down notes when Hess was highlighted. The librarian never once asked my interest in Nazi's so I don't know what she thought about my requests. Prepare yourself for a history lesson son," Stated like a wise old professor Theo thought.

"Students of Nazi history and in particular Rudolf Hess are caught between fact and fiction, both intertwining and overlapping. It is generally assumed that Hess was on a secret mission either ordered by Hitler or done entirely on his own; nothing definitive about that. Historians built cases based on the evidence they found for either theory. There's no doubt Hess took off from the Ausburg Airdrome in Germany, the flight plan kept to himself, bound for Scotland. Evidence released much later asserted Hess was actually on a peace mission in that May of 1941. The best and brightest historians maintained the mission was undertaken to convince England to stay out of the war, allowing the Germans to turn their mighty army east destroying Bolshevism in the Soviet Union. He did parachute to earth, he did fly in a Messerschmitt 110D and his plane crashed exactly twelve miles short of his destination, the Duke of Hamilton's estate.

"When word reached high officials in Germany about the flight Hitler declared Hess insane, a complete madman. It was reported he was furious discovering what Hess had done, purportedly telling his aides he'd wished the damn Brits had shot him down. Other's still believe it was all an act, a way for Hitler to disown the failed mission and save face.

"There are more unanswered questions about Hess than about any other person or situation in World War Two, with the exception of Hiroshima. One large question then and now is, was Hitler in on the plot? Both men are long dead but the relationship between Hitler and Hess was intimate so one can only assume Hitler gave his blessing for the journey.

"There's great mystery shrouding many of the actual facts, many still sealed up tightly by the British and not to be opened for another twenty years. Some facts however are undisputable and I say that because I was an eye witness. Hess used a false name, Albert Horn but I can't tell you if a real Albert Horn ever existed."

Glancing out the front door during pauses Theo caught site of Dr. Joan and Noah running, net poised to catch a butterfly. Each time the pair were spied tears welled in his eyes, blaming it on peat smoke when Sander asked if he was alright.

"After the war and the Nazi trials I became driven to learn more about the mysterious Rudolf Hess. Why? It was like an addiction I couldn't kick, certain my life would be different if he'd only crashed thirty miles from here. I'd spent no more than eight or ten hours with him but I felt I came to know him. I learned later he was interrogated by experts including Churchill. He was imprisoned in the Tower of London for much of the war, considered an enemy combatant. Few people were privy to how he managed those nearly five years or what Hess might have discussed. Tired of reading about the war the world moved on and Hess disappeared behind fortified walls, never to be a free man again.

"Getting my hands on all the literature I could find about Hess enabled me to learn about the powerful positions he held for many years in Nazi Germany. Whatever information the British authorities gleaned when he was their prisoner is sadly still state secret to this day, the records and notes during his years in the Tower still classified. Evidence points to a journey carefully planned, not the work of a mad man many espoused, carried out to prove to the Fuhrer the plan was essential to Hitler's new Germany.

"There're also many other unresolved issues because few historians have been privileged to read the notes from the various interrogations. A few years ago someone broke into a building where secreted World War two documents were kept. Some of the notes were leaked to a newspaper reporting Hess was aware of Hitler's plans to attack the Soviet Union, creating a two front-war. Hess believed it would lead to the destruction of the Third Reich. For certain however, is the incredible journey he made."

Hours later Noah and Dr. Joan returned looking quite happy, a dozen large butterflies in a glass bottle. Noah had a proud look on his face as did Dr. Joan. Finally something to be thankful for Theo said under his breath. Sander suggested freeing the butterflies so they could join their friends and family. Noah nodded and it was done. After lunch the pair went out once again to search for the largest butterfly in all of Scotland. Unbeknownst to Noah the time with Dr. Joan was his introduction to therapy. Adding peat bricks to the fire signaled it was time to resume Sander's tale.

"In reality I was a tiny cog in one of the greatest mysteries of World War Two. Beginning with his most unexpected visit and the ensuing chaos, Hess became part of my life. I never claimed to be an expert on the man but I know certain things others could not guess. Trying to discover truths became an obsession and for better or worse, he's been on my mind for forty years. With his death I hope it's finally the right time to put him on the back shelf.

"I'm actually rather fascinated by his life and exploits and I admit I'm persistent, searching for tiny bits of information often driving me mad. The British are a roadblock to many of the notes I would have liked to have read, protecting Hess' secrets for good reasons no doubt. Every now and then I was able to get hold of newly released papers from the British archives. In the last batch it was reported Hess displayed signs of instability even before his ill-fated flight. If there was something odd about Hess I simply attributed it to the extreme stress and ordeal of abandoning an aircraft, never having jumped before. I never suspected I was dealing with someone daft because given the circumstances he actually seemed quite logical. When Churchill heard about the capture he ordered no interrogations, treating Hess like a high profile prisoner of war.

"When word got back to Germany Hitler disowned Hess. Spells of disorientation, staring blankly off into space and acting odd Hitler screamed. Theo, the man I saw seemed reasonably sane and sensible. After his flight psychologists in Germany described him as completely mad, although never explaining how a disturbed individual could have managed such a difficult undertaking. When a number of prominent Nazis were put on trial in Nuremberg, Hess was deemed a special case. His first appearance told volumes about a man losing touch with the world. Whether it was fakery or a brilliant disguise, that's also secreted information. It was noted at the trials Hess slipped into bouts of amnesia, seemingly not recognizing his fellow Nazi's on trial.

"During the trial psychologists continued to examine Hess, concluding he suffered from a true psychoneurosis, primarily the hysterical type, partly genuine and genially faked."

Asking Sander to pause the story for a while Theo wanted to go outdoors hoping to join Dr. Joan and Noah before it got too dark. There was no sign of them but he was pleased that Noah was spending the day in Dr. Joan's world. For a brief moment he thought wouldn't it be something if Noah returned speaking.

When it was time for afternoon tea Sander said sit tight he'd be back in a few minutes. The few minutes turned into twenty allowing Theo to return to the doorway to watch the wayward pair. Cradling a canvas bag in his arms wrapped in heavy tape, Sander's face suggested he could be holding the Holy Grail. Slowly pulling layers of tape away he announced with some drama, what do we have here?"

Sander swore he'd only looked inside the bag once, a few days after Hess was led away by British authorities. "By the way at the conclusion of the Nuremburg Trials Hess was spared the death sentence and received life in prison. Why not the death penalty that many of his colleagues were handed? That's a question that might not have an answer.

"What I'm going to show you was a gift from the airman, that being Hess of course. It was possibly a thank you for my kindness and the offer of a warm home after his long ordeal."

Sander continued to pull strips of tape from the bag making Theo suspect it had to be extremely fragile. Possibly insignias, a Nazi flag or a weapon he thought? Painstakingly with gentle tugs Sander pulled a flight jacket out of the bag, proudly reporting it was the jacket Hess wore on his flight to Scotland.

"I told the airman I couldn't accept it but he insisted, cautioning me to keep it in a safe place because it could be quite valuable one day.

"When the British authorities searched my place their mission was to remove anything related to Hess' visit, taking such seemingly innocuous items as the mug Hess drank tea from. Several soldiers remained outside sifting through the wrecked remains of Hess' plane, picking the area clean like vultures, leaving not a single bolt or screw behind."

Holding the jacket up both men were taken aback. It was far too small to have fit Hess they both immediately realized. It might fit Noah, certainly not an adult Theo whispered. When Sander shook it out spiders and mold spores flew about the room. The small jacket was in remarkably good shape, Sander holding it to his face inhaling deeply.

"Sorry Sander but that can't be the actual flight jacket Hess wore so what do you make of it now?" There was no answer, Sander looking forlorn.

"I've seen photos of German World War Two airmen and this appears to be a typical World War Two standard issue flight jacket. I hid it away more than forty years ago but never examined it closely, never trying it on. From time to time I looked to make sure it was still safe but never holding it. I've kept that jacket under wraps all these years often thinking I probably should have turned it over to the British authorities. Handing the jacket to Theo Sander asked him to look it over.

Theo ran his fingers over the fabric, reaching into the pockets, lightly touching the insignias, patches and the black metal buttons.

"Don't touch the zipper" Sander cautioned. "I think it's pretty shot." Handing the jacket back to Sander Theo said the only thing unusual thing was it's child like size but other than that it was in good shape, a collector's treasure.

"I just created another mystery I'd actually been sitting on for a very long time" Sander said sadly. "Theo when Hess had his preliminary physical exam before being imprisoned in the Tower of London the records revealed to the public stated he was nearly six feet tall, weighing one hundred and sixty pounds, just about your proportions. When I first laid eyes on him his physical appearance was that of an average adult male. I guessed we were about the same size.

"This is the flight jacket Hess handed me and I would have bet the farm it was his own personal jacket. The crazy thing now is, if this did not actually belong to Hess who did it belong to?"

Theo didn't know what to say. "Think about this Theo. Is it possible there was second person on that plane, a passenger and thus not a solo flight as the world was told? When Noah returns I'd like to have him try it on. Just curious."

"Sander from what you observed when you met him do you think Hess was looking for a passenger, possibly a young child trapped in the wreckage? Do you think that's what he was looking for? Do you suppose it was a gift meant for the Duke of Hamilton? Do you know if the Duke had any young children? Did you see a second chute?"

Sander shook his head, no.

Chapter Twelve

Eager to hear Dr. Joan's first impression and thoughts about Noah it was time to push Hess aside. "I need to spend some time with Dr. Joan so would you mind looking after Noah for a bit so we can talk alone" he begged of Sander.

Sitting outside on a couple of boulders Theo got right to the point, asking if there was any hope of a recovery. Glancing inside watching Noah working with his sketch pad and colored pencils, the boy looked normal but stoic. The jar of butterflies was empty.

"There's many reasons for childhood trauma as we discussed but sadly this one is particularly cruel. Trauma creates great confusion in a child's mind making him or her unable to comprehend the feelings of unexpected and sudden loss. Given Noah's vacant stare it's as if he's lost in a forest with no way out.

"Grieving on the inside always leads to changes on the outside, thus the mutism but I caution you we'll have to be patient. There's no doubt in my mind Noah wants to be rid of his fears and return to the life he used to have, not an easy task. Keep this in mind. It's impossible to get the old life back because nobody can change what happened. Noah needs therapeutic help but on the positive side he's perceptive and able to figure out how to capture butterflies almost down to a science, so I believe he has the ability to work through this. If someone breaks a leg they use crutches. Therapy provides mental crutches making life a bit easier.

"You both experienced the tragic collapse of a once happy and functioning family. A large part of the healing process is learning how to deal with that loss and the subsequent life changes. There are several clinics in the states, some quite groundbreaking and Noah would do well in any of them. There's one in particular however I thought you might consider.

"Noah's reaction to the traumatic event is certainly the cause of his silence. It's not a physical ailment but there could be other issues. At times its difficult identifying children needing help because they display no symptoms. The silence might be a blessing in disguise right now because it illuminates a great problem. If Noah hadn't shut down you might not have become aware of problems. Untreated trauma impacts mental and physical development which I'm sure you're aware of.

"We don't want Noah's situation turning into a lifelong chronic condition and there's no time to waste. When the lives of family members are suddenly torn apart nothing in the world seems safe. The question becomes, how and when is the right time to discuss the tragedy with Noah? I'm certain you've done your best to avoid that talk and it's okay for now.

"Children Noah's age are mentally and emotionally maturing but very unable to cope with tragedy. They haven't yet developed coping mechanisms to deal with trauma so it's up to professionals to help them along. It's impossible for Noah to find words to describe how he feels, as if he'd have to learn a foreign language. Fostering a strong sense of safety and open communication is critical and remember this. Children get their cues from parents so you'll also need to get help for yourself.

"We've learned much about childhood trauma, discovering better methods to help facilitate breakthroughs all the time. Professionals with the right tools can identify the child's immediate need during the early session, that's why I'm so disappointed you didn't get the answers you sought. Is there only one method to treat everyone? No but each child experiencing what you and Noah are going through doesn't mean that you can't eventually lead healthier lives. There are services available for victims and families and I'll go over those with you when you return home. The opportunities to assess and repair are rather unique and that brings me to what I alluded to earlier. I can't do much for Noah here but the institute where I work does pioneering work with childhood traumas. I think Noah would be a an excellent candidate."

"How can I find out if the institute could work with us"?

"I'll give you an answer shortly."

"Trauma survivors carry a scar with them the rest of their lives so the goal is to make life healthy and manageable. It can often be a chronic condition people learn to deal with. When individuals especially children come face to face with unanticipated and overwhelming danger they become withdrawn and terrified. It's the same old story; fight or flight and we know which path Noah chose. If I were his therapist I'd treat him for an anxiety disorder which is very treatable in long term therapy. If you want the best professionals I'd recommend a colleague of mine, Dr. Stanley Becker who's had great success with children very much like Noah. Not coincidently I just so happen to work for him. I counsel children at a Connecticut residential treatment center called the High Meadows School. I'd be more than happy to have you visit when you're home and I could walk you through the course of treatment Noah might receive. I'm often recruited at twice the salary to work with different institutes but I stay there because of Dr. Becker. I would always be available to Noah if you wished.

"The boy is dealing with a situation very few people outside war zones experience in their young lives. Dr. Becker runs the facility, a residential center highly regarded for it's success with children displaying depression and negative self images. He's extremely compassionate and driven to do whatever's necessary to create a break through, quite often what others deem impossible. High Meadows would be an ideal place for Noah but before you make any decision there is one thing to consider. Entering any residential treatment center requires separation from family for periods of time. There are other treatment centers strictly outpatient but I truly believe this is your best option. Think about residential care because I believe it works best. I'm here another two days and then I'll be off exploring the north country."

Chapter Thirteen

The sky grew dark portending a risky drive back to the inn. Too many drivers spent the late afternoon at the pub Sander warned, becoming nuisances on the road. Fortunately the road was deserted. Noah, Joan and Theo ate dinner at the inn, the plan Theo would return to Sander's late morning alone. Dr. Joan agreed to be with Noah for the day so she might do counseling. The boy smiled hearing he'd spend time with Dr. Joan.

There was praise for the inn's food, courtesy of Greta and husband Franz. Over dinner they discussed butterflies and Nessie the Lock Ness Monster, nothing profound with Noah present. Dr. Joan said she didn't need her car the next day because she and Noah would be going on a long exploratory hike. Noah's smiles were becoming quite noticeable, something giving Theo another ounce of hope. After desert Noah fell immediately asleep, an early bed time for a very tired little boy.

The next day morning Theo drove to Sander's in the rental, the separation from Noah feeling very strange. Dr. Joan made High Meadows sound like an ideal place for the therapy Noah sensed, getting the help he desperately needed. The big question was, could he survive alone without him? There had always been hope before seeing other doctors, each sadly ending in disappointment. Was separation a good thing or would it plunge Noah deeper into the shell protecting him he wondered?

As usual a warm peat fire was burning at Sander's place and the never endless cups of hot brewed Scottish tea. Sander got right to something he'd wanted to ask before returning to his tale. "An old busy-body wants to know if there's something going on between you and the doc."

Theo laughed, replying they were just recent acquaintances and saying that put a mischievous look on Sander's grizzly face. The twinkle in is eyes told him he couldn't fool the old man. Time to disclose the real purpose of her visit he decided.

"Sander, Dr. Joan is an exceptionally fine children's therapist I happened to meet quite accidentally on the plane ride here. Seeing your silly grin I assure you there's nothing going on between us. Now if you'd like to begin where we left off, I've got the day to myself."

Sander picked up where he'd left off, the story he referred to as the tale of the man who fell to earth on his farm. The words as usual were transfixing and absorbing, Sander a natural born story teller. It was nearly impossible not to fall under his spell. It was one of the rare times Noah wasn't by his side, feeling as if part of him was missing. He was happy the boy was safe and certainly appearing to have a great time. The separation would be much worse if Sander's tales weren't so damn riveting he acknowledged.

"The people of Eaglesham have no idea what happened on my farm, not an inkling but if they did it was never brought up. A few villagers like me were trained to watch the skies for German aircraft. Due to Hess' unusual and erratic flight path however his plane managed to avoid detection. In the years that have passed I've kept the entire incident to myself, mostly because of the threats I'd received from the Brits. And besides, the entire incident made no sense to me so how could I explain it to others. Weeks and then months passed after the incident while it became a recurring bad dream. How might I explain what happened and sound sane? Deep inside I was a mess though, an uneasiness lodged in my head. As an aside it's never really gone away. It's the pea under the mattress syndrome keeping me awake most nights. If you read the history of World War Two you and the rest of the world would learn Rudolf Hess brought a secret message to the British. After his capture not more than one hundred meters from here the world heard nothing about the man until he went on trial at Nuremberg.

Long after the trial ended he simply became a footnote in World War Two history. Sadly, Hess has taken up permanent residence in my head.

"It was quite surprising discovering the jacket was child size but believe it or not it touched something inside me. This might be extremely preposterous but I don't believe it was ever meant to be a gift. Don't ask me why because I really can't give you a good answer although there has to be a hidden meaning attached. In hindsight I wished I'd declined the offer or passed it along to the British soldiers, sorry I didn't think of that. Hess certainly was not wearing this jacket when he fell to earth so what I'm thinking right now is pure Sander speculation and probably a million miles from the truth. Suppose there was someone else on that plane? By the way I did some research into my old neighbor the Duke. He had no children, no heirs and his place today is a fancy bed and breakfast. Who owned this jacket? Hess spent a great deal of time sifting through the wreckage and the surrounding area claiming he was looking for something important. Last night I woke in a fitful sweat, solely focused on what the significance of that damn jacket is.

"I remind myself often I was an witness to one of the strangest oddities of World War Two. I've spent more than half my life going over and over the events of that day, beating myself up relentlessly.

"I'd like to go over this again if you don't mind to see if I've been overlooking something. Here's what I know and what I don't know. On May 10, 1941 Hess piloted his plane on a course to Scotland. It was his personal aircraft allegedly training often when the weather was good. His supposed mission was the opportunity to visit with the Duke of Hamilton but it never took place, believing the Duke would be sympathetic to his peace plan. He also believed the Duke was prominent in his opposition to the British government's war plans, seeing an opening others did not.

"Hess was arrested right in front of my eyes and then flown away and held in isolation in British custody until the end of the war. In 1946, I forget the exact month he was returned to Germany to stand trial in Nuremberg with other major Nazi war criminals. There was no mention of a passenger on that flight in any of the testimony, nor even a hint or rumor of an extra jacket brought along.

"At the end of the trial Hess was convicted of crimes against peace and conspiracy to create war. He and others spared the death penalty were transported to Spandau Prison in western Berlin where Hess spent the rest of his life in a solitary cell. In time the world eventually forgot about him. He became the sole prisoner at Spandau when others served their terms or died, the four powers the United States, Great Britain, France and the Soviet Union deciding he'd remain there until the day he died.

"His death has created more new mysteries and opened old wounds. At the old age of 93 his passing was announced with little fanfare but after word got out it quickly became a momentous event. He'd allegedly hung himself but doubters insist he was murdered for fear he would reveal certain poisonous facts about his exploit. After his death the prison was demolished preventing it from becoming a neo-Nazi shrine.

"Thanks to freedom of information acts passed in Parliament a few years ago we know more about the man but we still don't know the entire story. I know there's more to Hess' life and there are things we'll never learn and sadly I can't live with that reality. He saw himself as an envoy, visibly shocked when the British held him as a prisoner of war, always claiming he journeyed at great risk to broker a peace creating a united front against Bolshevism.

"Little more to tell for now I guess. Read about him when you get home if you're interested. He was certainly a close confidant of Hitler and whether he knew about Hitler's plan to attack the Soviet Union or not, the world has not reached the end of the long story. The peace mission was a gamble, the goal save Germany."

Chapter Fourteen

Theo was elated seeing Dr. Joan on the sofa by the fire at the inn, a glass of white wine in her hand. Noah lay next to her sound asleep.

"I must have tired Noah out but it was a great day."

Theo wasn't sure if the peat fire made him uncomfortably warm or if it was the moment.

Thanking Dr. Joan for taking Noah under her wing again he apologized for making her work on vacation. "You're actually helping two very lost souls," his words making him teary.

Sleep was hard to come by that night, sorry he hadn't been more open with Sander about the tragedy. Looking for the morning Glasgow newspaper outside the door there was an envelope instead. It was from Dr. Joan.

'I want you to fully understand that what young Noah is experiencing is temporary and treatable. As a therapist I'm very familiar with childhood trauma and I don't give up until there's a breakthrough. Don't you ever give up for a minute because this doctor says he's going to be okay.

'Years ago I had a patient who'd suddenly stopped talking after her father died in an accident at work. Her distraught mother told me at one time they couldn't stop her from talking. She's not talking at all now said the mother. Very similar to what Noah is experiencing.

'When I got into this profession fifteen years ago there was very little information available about sudden silences caused by trauma. It's a rather rare phenomena unlike crying or acting out when lives fall apart. I once attended a conference in Geneva where doctors and scientists discussed these types of children's trauma cases. It didn't take long for everyone to see the common underlying thread. Studies highlight the underlying depression and survivor's guilt sometimes hidden, usually associated with soldiers on the battlefield. Studies done by a German research team were the first to link childhood silence to anxiety. Treat the anxiety and we get results. There's much to learn but we've come a long way.

'There are many reasons for selective-muteness but doctors concur it's anxiety based. Every child is different and no one shoe fits all but we've discovered the common denominator. What Noah's experiencing was once considered untreatable, given time the child will eventually speak experts said. Children with selective-muteness often open up to other children and not adults. At High Meadows we place children into small therapy groups and we've had great success.

'Noah needs to be in a setting offering full time treatment and that takes time and unfortunately money. I know it was difficult for you to rehash the tragic events of that day but I'm gratified you were able to do it. What happened inside Noah when he learned about the deaths was overload. Selective-muteness varies from child to child but the underlying causes are similar. It's not too late because from our day together he's still at the crossroad and recovery is possible. Quick action is needed however.

'Noah hasn't been able to adapt to the new life since the accident and who could blame him. His innocence and childhood were damaged by the upsetting words from the police officers. Do traumatic events in children cause selective-muteness in everyone? No, there are many different reactions to trauma but there is one common relief and that can be found in a residential setting. Noah should also have a complete physical exam soon because such maladies as hearing loss can't entirely be ruled out. There could be a hidden physical ailments a doctor might detect. If you decide upon the residential clinic it doesn't have to be High Meadows but

I believe it's the best in the country for what ails Noah. I can do all the footwork and all you'd have to do is get Noah there for an intake interview and exam. Joan'

Fourteen

Berlin Germany May 10, 1941

The handwritten note was found on Hess's desk the evening of his journey. It was redacted and the world soon became privy to a carefully edited version.

'To my future heirs I did not choose God like the early apostles, instead God chose me. I will not arrive at what might be my final destination in life without fears but I have overcome them. Dreams of endless lines of children's coffins with weeping mothers troubles me greatly.

'German heroes spring from the essence of the German people, a true leader able to withstand the challenges of difficult times. This all springs from our enigmatic leader, my Fuhrer Adolf Hitler. My place and time on this earth has not ended so I ask for your patience. At times threads in a masterpiece can seemingly be broken forever but I insist they can be carefully knitted back together. The reasons for my journey few will truly understand. Confronted by a very hard decision it was the most testing time of my life. How often has my Fuhrer said let no one judge my decisions because my actions are always correct. I know what I am doing is right and the future will prove it so.

'The doubters listen to everyone's opinion and become spiteful. I simply ask not to be judged unfairly. The outside world has no idea Germany is moving toward a war in the East it cannot win. Herr Hitler listened carefully to my advice but dismissed me. I have always worked to please him so this was very difficult. Do not judge me harshly with your words but by your thoughtful hearts. I was permitted to work for many years of my life under the greatest son Germany brought forth. My mission is not wanderlust but the action of a good and noble German soldier.

'When this note is read I trust my flying skills will have me soaring over the Rhine and across the North Sea. With my trusted maps and charts I shall be watchful, flying over largely unfamiliar terrain. God is not my only co-pilot.'

Chapter Fifteen

Sander read the note highlighted in a history book about World War Two. The last words took his breath away.

"To me those closing words could be the proverbial sore thumb, the neon light illuminating a foggy evening. I wonder why others haven't made something of these curious words. God is not my only co-pilot raises a red flag for me. I don't know for certain if there was a passenger on board but this gives me more pause to consider it.

"Theo I won't keep you here much longer because you've got to get home and I've got some work to do. I'll miss you, praying you'll be safe and hoping you might travel this way again. There's always going to be a warm peat fire going no matter where I am and of course, good conversation. I wish you the very best for yourself and Noah, the young lad I've become especially fond of."

The time with Sander had truly been an amazing journey Theo could never have imagined. He'd learned about the McCann's and the airman who fell from the sky one innocent day. It was quite a journey because Dr. Joan also came into his life very unexpectedly.

Sander looked exhausted when Theo said goodbye. He was concerned about leaving him alone, knowing he bore a heavy burden. He knew he should stay but that was impossible.

Over dinner with Dr. Joan he said the words he once thought impossible. Whatever was best for Noah including separation although troublesome was necessary.

Saying goodbye to Sander weighed on his mind, thinking about the hours listening to a most remarkable tale, a truly haunting experience. Despite the long distance from the States he promised himself he'd be back.

There were no more Rudolf Hess tales just Sander's final request Theo learn more about the famous Nazi while home. Noah would miss Sander and of that he was certain but as Sander told the boy, they all had work to do and had to get on with their lives. The sad reality Sander would be alone in the world made it extremely difficult to walk away.

He gushed words of heartfelt thanks to Dr. Joan for going out of her way to work with Noah. He could not help think about her as a true saint. The difficult decision regarding separation was not easy but he was convinced it was the right thing for Noah. He thanked Dr. Joan for her generous offer to look into High Meadows and to arrange an admission interview. The words Noah was a proper candidate for the type of treatment the center provided felt like a warm blanket on a cold dark night. Dr. Joan said she'd already called Dr. Becker with news of a possible new admission.

She poked her head out the window on her rental wishing them both luck. Looking directly at Noah Dr. Joan she said she expected to see him in a few days. Holding a book out the window made the boy react with disbelief; the title A Scottish Butterfly Afraid of Flying.

Noah and Theo had been away from home for nearly eight days and as the hours dwindled before their departure flight, Theo wondered if he and Noah would ever feel comfortable in their own home again. It held bittersweet memories and the kicker, it was a place without a warm peat fire making life better.

The flight was uneventful, Theo working on a long heartfelt letter to Doctor Joan with snippets about Noah he wanted her to know. Re-reading

95

the letter brought up nostalgic feelings. He wanted her to learn more about Noah before the tragedy.

Walking into their home Theo felt sad because it wasn't home anymore but a house. Mentally and physically spent, he got Noah back into is bedtime routines meaning returning to his own room and bed. Next to Noah's bed was his brother's empty bed. Gathering Noah up into his arms he carried him to his bedroom. One tiny hand held on to Theo, the other holding the diagram of the McCann family tree.

The first few days home were a blur, catching up on mail and phone calls to High Meadows asking questions whenever they popped into his head. A date had not been set for an interview but Theo was assured it would be soon.

Preparing Noah for another session with another care giver wasn't easy but this time there would be a welcoming face. Even though he trusted Dr. Joan he and Noah had gone through the process with other counselors many times with no success. The sessions always began with Noah by his side until an aide came to take him to a play area so the counselor could talk to Theo alone. Each new appointment began with hope but in the back of his mind sat the dreary thought of another rejection. Told each time there was not much the professionals could do but wait it out felt like a dagger plunged deep into his heart.

Theo's nerves could easily be riled, especially when he mistakenly drove too close to the intersection where the accident occurred. A sound from Noah's throat made him realize where they were in time to make an illegal u-turn.

The call from High Meadows about a date finally came. Could he bring Noah to the center at nine in the morning on a Friday in six days. Asking if he should pack a suitcase for Noah the assistant director said he would not be staying after the meeting. It was merely an evaluation to make sure Noah could handle the situation.

Time stood still waiting for the time and date of the intake meeting, days filled with hope and despair. Noah was still not speaking, each day making the situation feel more permanent. Theo asked Noah more yes and no questions hoping one word would crack the shell. Shall we read a different book tonight? No response.

Hearing Dr. Joan's voice on the phone melted some of the ice. "Have Noah here at nine and remember it's just an evaluation. It takes about three hours but not to worry. Noah has actually already been accepted on my say so but he still has to go through the entire interview process.

The furthest thing from Theo's mind was Scotland and Rudolf Hess until he found a letter in his mail box, return address Sander.

'Hope you had a good trip home and that you and Noah are settling in. My heartfelt thanks for putting up with an old windbag during your stay. What we discussed I'd kept to myself for more than forty years and although it was bittersweet recalling that day it revealed how much my life has changed. I can't thank you enough for being with me. My best to the boy. Any interest in pursuing the elusive Mr. Hess? Stay well, Sander.'

Chapter Sixteen

The day finally arrived for the one hour drive to the school in South Woodstock, Connecticut, not quite fifty miles from home. Theo wondered if it was a hospital, a school with dorms or an old Victorian mansion the town was noted for. Sitting in the waiting area he was handed a stack of pamphlets describing the various treatments provided by the institute.

'Welcome to High Meadows School' was the first one, followed by a pamphlet describing selective-muteness. 'My name is Doctor Stanly Becker, the institute's founder and director. I have the pleasure of letting you know why this is such a very special place for children. We offer a variety of effective treatments for many neurosis and the underlying issues affecting children's lives. I have a Ph.D in clinical child psychology from Yale University, my emphasis children. Most of my staff have been here for many years, each with advanced degrees in child care. We provide children with treatments based on evidence-based approaches, specializing in a range of issues including autism spectrum disorders, behavior challenges, ADHD, learning difficulties and developmental delays. We proudly lead the field in the treatment of selective-muteness.

'It's normal for all children and adults to be shy in certain circumstances but when the shyness is so extreme it stops a person from ever speaking, it becomes a psychosis.

'Patient Jane eight years old sang and danced in front of her family but in music class she was paralyzed with fear, unable to say a word. She came to us for treatment and in time returned to her chatty self.'

'Patient James, nine years old used to banter with his soccer mates but stopped speaking entirely after the death of an older sister. He simply stared off into space on the soccer pitch, silent and withdrawn. After treatment he can't stop talking.

'Everyone becomes quiet from time to time and sometimes it's very useful because it protects us from doing things that may be embarrassing or awkward. When silence keeps a child from speaking in normal situations, the term selective-muteness is applied.

'Children with selective mutism have not consciously stopped talking. Non-speaking becomes a way for them to protect themselves from the severe anxiety that overcame them. Because anxiety is the root of selective mutism, pressuring the child to speak can often make them more anxious. We set no time limits on treatment.

'Parents play a large role in the recovery process working with us hand in hand creating a healthy and safe environment. A child feels safe when we replace the child's anxiety with the right tools designed to help them heal. The first therapy sessions are to make the child feel well protected and taken care of. We talk to the child about their specific situations using small steps, not to entirely eliminate the anxiety but to make it manageable.

'When a child or an adult faces unpleasantness often the most common reaction is fight or flight. The root cause is something so frightening most survive by fleeing. We teach our patients how to fight.

'The longer mutism continues the more difficult it becomes to change behaviors. What the child is experiencing is essentially a mental breakdown, something many believe only affects adults. You and I don't have to understand all of a child's feelings but they are all acknowledged here.

'There are mental health professionals on call or on duty twenty-four hours a day. We employ psychologists, speech language therapists, psychiatrists and medical doctors. We demand the parents get involved with the child's treatment and healing process.

"The staff at High Meadows works very hard to create a stress-free environment, encouraging children to have contact with other patients. That interaction greatly increases the likelihood a child might open up to someone like them.

"Medications might be useful in some cases for children who do not respond well to our intervention program. Antidepressants known as SSRIs help reduce anxiety and in good faith, we never medicate without a consult and an okay from parents and medical doctor.

'New patients will immediately recognize they're in an environment surrounded with comfort. Checkers and other board games are useful tools because words are not required. We'll try to get a child to make gestures or write but we won't push if there's resistance. In time simple yes or no answers to questions will be a breakthrough. Do you like pizza for example might generate a nod but hopefully in time a vocal yes or no. As treatment progresses our staff begins to ask open ended questions such as what is your favorite meal. We expect our children to vocalize their thoughts and feelings only when they are ready. Children develop from within. Breaking down the wall of silence is a formidable task.'

"High Meadows is first and foremost a stabilizing center and where the child goes from here is well planned. We never give up until we find the best way to put cracks in the wall. The emphasis is helping every child find a way to escape the wilderness he or she's grown comfortable with.

'We have special room for new patients, places where the child might hear familiar sounds and see familiar things. Each room is personalized to the child's tastes and provides a key to help them escape from their prison of uncertainties, anxieties and fears.'

That was as far as Theo got before he and Noah were escorted into Dr. Becker's office. The walk reminded him of his first day at school as a young boy, filled with nervous energy. All life's burdens were suddenly released because in the room with Dr. Becker was Saint Joan of Arc.

Chapter Seventeen

The trip home was trying, Theo fearing he'd break down sobbing. Noah had not said a word but there was solace not having the punched in the gut feeling at the end of a meeting. Noah was accepted into High Meadows, a starting date when a bed opened up. Dr. Joan was truly a sight for tired and weary eyes, an angel and a true saint. Before leaving Noah threw his arms tightly around her waist.

Noah will succeed Theo believed because he had a special friend at a special place. At the end of the interview Dr. Joan said I'd like to stop by your place after Noah goes to bed tonight to give you some insights as to how best to prepare yourself for the separation. I sense your deep disquiet. Theo smiled, thinking the tide might slowly be turning.

Nerves were still as taut as a guitar string most of the time, but life seemed a bit more manageable after the intake work. When the doorbell rang that evening Theo prayed it was the beginning of a new day. It was their new saint.

Chatting about Scotland and great uncle Sander brought back good and bad feelings. Mercifully Hess had graciously taken leave from his mind, a nice break.

Sporting a grey tartan tweed dress and tam, the spirit of Scotland lived on Theo announced upon her arrival. Before sitting down she asked if she might peek in at Noah. Standing in the doorway for several long minutes, Theo became overcome with gratitude.

"I spoke with Dr. Becker about Noah for nearly two hours after you left so I'm going to tell you a little about the director. He's an exceptionally thoughtful person with a heart of pure gold. When he finished seeing your son he told me he was certain Noah could work with us. When Noah was escorted to the playroom the clinician with him never took her eyes off him. Her report stated the boy looked sure of himself and interested in the various toys and books in the room. The clinician asked Noah if he'd like other children to come to his special room to play. He shook his head, telling us he wasn't ready for companionship yet.

"Many children entering the activity room for the first time often simply stand there, staring but not seeing. Noah focused on several items in the room right away, particularly the books.

"When Dr. Becker got the observation report he was quite pleased, saying the boy would be an excellent candidate for High Meadows. If Noah were able to catch hold of a tiny thread he said it would begin the process of unraveling what was going on in his silent world."

The two spoke for nearly an hour about Noah until there was no more to say. Their conversation then turned to their interests in music, art, literature, movies and travels. The conversation stopped when Noah began stirring. When it appeared he'd gone back to sleep Dr. Joan said it was a good time to go.

"Feel free to call me anytime either at work or home and Theo make sure you take time to treat yourself well. You're not responsible for what happened and neither is Noah. As to how you're managing I'd very much like you to see a therapist, someone who can steer you down the difficult road you're traveling. I'll give you a few names, good people who'll understand the heavy load you're carrying. It's important to be ready when Noah speaks again and he will."

Several days passed without a call until late one afternoon he heard the words a bed had opened up.

"Have Noah here between ten and eleven. Do you have any questions?" Theo had scores but they could wait.

Chapter Eighteen

Noah acted like a brave soldier when Theo dropped the boy off. A kiss and hug and the words he was very proud of his son were said without tears from either. Later he would admit he wanted to pull Noah into his arms and run as far from High Meadows as possible. As long as it takes became his mantra, hoping he'd have the strength to believe that. Noah will eventually speak again Dr. Joan insisted, time not being an issue.

When Doctor Joan greeted Noah she had a book in her hands, a welcoming gift titled The Magical Journey of the Curious Butterfly.

Feeling like a stranger walking back into his home, the nagging sense it was not a home but a house hit especially hard. Why did it have to happen he lamented? A near perfect life filled with love and happiness was gone. It was a home once he said aloud.

The next morning Theo reached across his bed to touch Noah and for a brief upsetting moment he realized he wasn't there. There was no reason to get up he reasoned, convinced he had not had a mental breakdown but was reeling from all the traveling and decisions made. The drop off a day earlier was bittersweet but that morning he only felt the bitterness. My life is in a freefall he groaned, wondering if talking to one's self was indeed a sign of mental illness.

When the noise in his head quieted it was pure relief, but the clatter never entirely went away. Desiring nothing more than to drive to the institute to see Noah and give him a bear hug and a kiss tortured him. It was a different kind of loneliness felt, one he didn't like and wasn't used to. He sensed his life was slowly slipping away, the sound of the doorbell saving further grief.

A package had been left on the front step, the delivery van driving away. Looking at the mailing label Theo saw it was from Scotland, return address Sander McCann. He thought it might be the family tweed jacket passed down through the generations of the McCann family, it's unique crest sewn on. Shaking the package it made no sound convincing him it was the jacket he'd eyed with reverence. Opening it in Noah's room brought on a sadness, thinking about Sander. He lay down on Noah's bed to close his weary eyes for a few minutes.

Hours later unsure of the time or the day he realized he'd slept for nearly two hours. He didn't remembered walking into Noah's room taking time to gather his wits.

He eyeballed the package with a bittersweet feeling. How many hours had he and Sander been together sharing the tale of the mysterious airman who fell to earth.

Snapping out of the fog took some effort, the walls of the room appearing to have moved in while he slept.

Removing tape from the package he pictured Sander in his familiar chair near the fire at that exact moment, struck with the thought that two very important people in his life were very far away.

Instead of the blazer there was a heavy woolen sweater he'd seen in one of the town's shops and admired. Holding it up to see if it were the right size he saw something else inside. It was the neatly folded child's flight jacket Sander received from the airman. The jacket had been hidden away for forty years so why was Sander parting with it now he wondered?

Tossing the sweater aside and holding the jacket up touching the insignias, badges, patches and rusted flight medals a cold chill ran through his body. It felt evil. Don't fool with the zipper he reminded himself. Holding it to his nose and inhaling deeply the smell of burnt peat and mold took him back to his special chair near the fireplace. Holding it against his body made one thing certain. It was a child's jacket, certainly not Hess' adding to an ongoing mystery. Was it a gift for the Duke of Hamilton? They'd kicked that thought around until discovering the Duke had no children. Could it actually have belonged to a passenger, perhaps a stowaway on Hess' airplane he wondered?

Removing one of Noah's winter coats from the closet Theo placed it on the bed, lying the flight jacket on top. Both jackets were very nearly the same exact size. Noah was normal height and weight for an eleven year old so ……….. He couldn't finish the thought. The flight jacket was certainly not Hess's, most likely crafted for a young boy or girl the same age and build as Noah. His mind was on fire wondering why Sander sent it along.

He walked from Noah's bedroom to the phone in a daze but once he held the phone he had no idea why he'd picked it up. To call Sander? To call High Meadows? To call Dr. Joan? Putting the phone down as if it might burn him he slumped down onto the living room sofa.

PART TWO

Chapter Nineteen

Waking early after another unsettled and fitful night the first thought was three days had passed since Noah started treatment. No phone calls from High Meadows or Dr. Joan added to the uneasiness impossible to shake. Told to expect little or no contact the first few days was emphasized with the words be patient until one of two things happen. One, if there's been be a classic breakthrough or two, Noah was miserable and wanted to come home.

Ignoring the regulations Theo drove straight to the institute, pacing the reception area like an expectant father. He was not alone he realized. A couple possibly in their mid twenties sat like zombies, anguished looks on their faces. They'd briefly looked up when Theo walked in, the disappointment on their faces saying it was not who they'd expected.

An aide came for the couple, the emotion so heavy the room felt as if it was a hundred degrees. Theo continued pacing, trying to take his mind off the world because it was strangling him. In a flash his mind pictured the airman who fell to the earth. Staring out the large picture window his mind and body were suddenly in Scotland, oblivious to the sound of someone entering the waiting room. Donna was the name on the badge, asking Theo to follow her to a room where he'd receive an update from Noah's team.

It was impossible to stay composed, walking not to a meeting but toward the edge of a cliff.

Like an angel descending from heaven Dr. Joan was there to give Theo a warm hug. "Let's get right down to business because this visit wasn't scheduled and many of us have to put our work aside. Actually Theo I thought you'd unexpectedly turn up a day ago." The staff laughed, the sound lifting some of the black cloud.

"Noah is doing as well as expected said the team leader, especially from someone away from home and family for the first time."

It was nothing to cheer about and then Dr. Joan took over the impromptu session "Noah had a fitful first night so I stayed with him, reading one of the books from our library until he fell asleep. Once during the night he got up and was found walking the hallway. An aide returned him to his room, tucked him in and sang quietly. He slept through the night waking to a big smile from the overnight aide. After dressing she brought him to his own personalized play room designed with objects you noted on the intake form.

"For a time he wouldn't look directly at any of the staff or his surroundings, but there were no overt signs of ill ease, eventually becoming curious. He was carefully observed to see how he'd interact with his new play things. The children's play rooms are all different, the one for Noah with butterflies on the walls, plants and adventure books. His first effort was to touch the butterflies suspended from the ceiling. There were no words spoken but there was a look of awe telling us he was pleased.

"In the afternoon on his first full day" Dr. Joan continued, "the team let him know there was another boy his age who had his own special playroom. Would he like to see the room or have the boy come visit his butterflies? Too my delight he nodded. Both children were diagnosed with selective-muteness yet they played with much animation, especially with a wooden train set.

"He's still living inside his protected armor but we see tiny cracks that should begin to free him eventually. Noah won't start group therapy for a week but in the meantime he'll be able to visit his personal play room anytime he wants. We always offer the opportunity to choose another boy so the two can play together, An aide always observes, writing notes for the staff to review in the evening. The first three days we asked questions requiring a yes or no answer with no expectation the child will suddenly speak.

"Treatment as I mentioned is often a slow prescribed process with no easy or overnight fixes. I can't tell you how long Noah will be here, definitely seven more days before he can go home for a visit. We're already seeing less anxious behaviors and that's a very positive sign."

"Can I see him" Theo asked?

"Let's hold off on that for now."

Not the reply Theo hoped for so Dr Joan explained why not. "Noah was able to say goodbye to you without any fuss the day you brought him here but seeing you this soon might cause a different reaction. He's in a good place right now both physically and mentally so let's not disrupt that. By the way, if I'd known you had thoughts about dropping in I would have done my best to discourage you.

"We'll have Noah another seven full days and I know that sounds like an eternity but be assured those days are most critical."

Seven more days Theo rued, feeling like a lifetime sentence. He dreaded going home without seeing Noah, returning to a place that used to be a home but now only a place to eat and sleep. Dr. Joan took Theo's hand and walked him to the exit. "I hope you understand not seeing him right now is in Noah's best interest. The look on Dr. Joan's face made him believe she could read minds.

Driving home Theo wondered if he was ready to drive through the intersection where the accident happened. He couldn't avoid it forever he told himself but not today he decided.

His house felt even more foreign, everything in it's proper place with the exception of Noah. The house was too cold and then it became too hot.

It was filled with light and then eerie darkness. Walking into Noah's bedroom and staring at the flight jacket he wondered again why Sander sent it along. He'd not thought about Sander or the airman during his visit to the institute and the sight of the jacket bewildered him.

What to do with the jacket he wondered? Why did Sander send it to him and not keep it or even turn it over to the authorities? Had something bad or unexpected happened to his uncle? The jacket would certainly be valuable to a collector but if word got back to Sander he'd sold it he'd be crushed. Why was it aboard Hess's airplane? Did it belong to a young boy or a girl, possibly thrown from the wreckage on impact, a child running frightened into the woods? Sander insisted he'd only seen one parachute but it was a windy day he acknowledged. If there was a passenger who didn't bail he or she could not have survived the crash, yet when he'd looked inside the wreckage there was no body. Was the owner of the flight jacket a stowaway unbeknownst to Hess? Was it meant to be a gift? If there was a passenger had British authorities located a possible second person and hidden him away?

Those questions had no answers but it allowed a little time to take his sorry mind off Noah. The Nazi jacket lying on Noah's bed was wrong he knew, something evil. What should I do with it said in despair? That could be decided with a phone call to Sander he figured.

It took forever to get the town hall phone number in Eaglesham, frustration building like a swollen dam. Compared to what Noah was going through the jacket was a minor annoyance he'd decided. When the phone rang across the ocean the sound made him feel close to Sander. The phone rang once and then twice, hope sinking with each subsequent ring like cold water pouring over him. The call went unanswered. Maybe it was for the best he whispered into the phone, feeling even sorrier for himself. He'd given it the good fight only to lose again. It was growing darker outside meaning with a five hour time difference in Eaglesham, it was late in the evening there so of course no one would be there to answer the phone. Get a grip on yourself he shouted angrily.

The jacket felt cursed, taunting him with the evil associated with it. He felt he'd lose the last bit of peace if it remained in his home.

CHAPTER TWENTY

Reminding himself of the time difference between home and Eaglesham, Theo called again. Praying the phone might be answered and to his surprise he heard a woman's voice. Without waiting for a hello he shouted in a surely tone, "I must speak with Sander McCann. This is his great nephew calling from America."

"May I help you" was the woman's response, noticeably unfriendly.

"No but if you'll put Mr. McCann on the phone I'd be greatly appreciative. This is Theo McCann his grand nephew.

"And" was her response?

"And If he can't come to the phone I ask would you please leave a message that I'd called just to check on him."

"What's your business with Mr. McCann "said gruffly?"

Theo felt the hairs on his neck stiffening.

"I recently spent eight days with him, much of it in the old McCann homestead. Perhaps he mentioned my name, Theo McCann? I was with my son Noah."

"I don't recall but then again Mr. McCann is a very private man. Are you certain I can't help you with something?"

The responses fueled an ongoing resentment. Don't be the ugly American he cautioned himself. Be tactful and speak in a gentler tone. "I really need to talk with my uncle."

"Mr. McCann is in a very important meeting right now and I just answer the phone when he's busy or out. When he's free I'll tell him his nephew called."

Sighing with frustration Theo added it was awfully important but not to let Sander know that. Vowing not to end the call until she assured him, the woman simply hung up.

Feeling as if he were in no man's land he had a thought he needed to talk with Dr. Joan. As to what he might say he truly had no clue, just needing to hear some optimism and reassurance in her words and voice. The call to the institute was as frustrating as the call to Scotland, told she was with a patient and would be tied up for a while. For the second time in the early morning another message was left. Zero for two he bemoaned.

He felt as he were a leaf twisting in the wind. Unpleasant thoughts made it seem like rush hour on an emotional turnpike. Aware he was edging closer to insanity, the walls were definitely closing in.

The phone rang, dissipating the poor me's away for a moment. Was it Dr. Joan or Sander, heads or tails? It was Dr. Joan.

Shaking the cobwebs from his aching head he asked how Noah was doing, his own voice unrecognizable. The words were said in desperation, wondering if Dr. Joan recognized someone drowning. Like a dam bursting he blurted out the reason for the call.

"I'm really very sorry to bother you but I need your professional advice. Do you have a few moments to spare?"

Dr. Joan chucked. "We met yesterday and you seemed strong so do you want to tell me what's going on right now?"

"I know that I'm not to have contact with Noah so that's not the reason for the call. I need your permission to leave the area for a while."

"Do me a favor Theo. Take five or ten deep breaths, get yourself comfortable and then get to the point. What's going on?"

"Here's the situation. There are six days remaining before the ten day session ends and I might have to return to Scotland to deal with possible trouble with Sander. I guess I'm asking would I be looking for trouble leaving the area and being a bit out of touch for a few days? I can give you a number where I could be reached at the inn." There was no immediate response.

"It's a rather touchy situation but since you know a little about Sander's story, it has to do with his obsession with Hess. I hate to say it but I believe it's killing him. I can't get in touch with him and my gut tells me he's either in trouble or sick. I've called many times and always told he's not available. I hate to drop this on you but I have a feeling something's not quite right. A visit could possibly help resolve two situations. One, it might allow me to take my mind off Noah for the next six days. I don't mean that in a bad way but I need time to pull myself together for Noah's sake. Secondly, I need to help Sander put Hess to rest. It's quickly sucking the life out of him and if I lose him I fear what that would do to Noah. Does my being away and possibly out of touch pose problems for you or Noah, or me?"

"If you're asking for my permission to take care of a personal situation you have my blessing. Noah is fine and I don't anticipate any issues arising. Parents sometimes show up at the oddest times because they're not convinced their child can function without them. A few arrive in the middle of the night wanting to rescue their child as if we were a cult, not a world class children' s treatment center. Noah and I have a special bond because of our time together in Scotland and knowing that it should make life easier for you. Noah seems very comfortable with me, a closeness usually not found until much later in treatment. Enjoy your time with Sander and please give him my best wishes. Anything else"?

The heartfelt words thank you Saint Joan of Ark seemed quite appropriate.

115

Chapter Twenty One

Theo continued calling the town hall to no avail, earning the wrath of Mrs. Tavish who referred to him as the great American pest. She claimed all the messages were delivered and if there was no response there was little more she could do. "You know you can lead a horse to water but you can't make it drink." In frustration Theo hung up without saying goodbye.

The day was becoming fanatical, nervously waiting for a return call from Sander that never came. To relieve the free floating uneasiness he picked up the manuscript of the book he'd been writing. After a few pages he realized he couldn't remember what he'd just written or even the character's names. The walls were practically touching him.

A quick trip to the town library to take his mind off Noah and Sander was a needed geographical cure. With Hess' recent death there was much new material available to the public. Copying obituaries and news items from all the library newspapers he would take and read them at home.

Several of the more prominent newspapers printed Hess stories on the front page. With other it took some searching. Most articles described his mysterious life from birth to death, without a single mention of the farmer or the place in Scotland where Hess first appeared. There was still a great deal of mystery surrounded the former Nazi, maybe even more since his death Theo realized from his reading.

Was it prudent to be three thousand miles from Noah? Even sixty miles away seemed foreboding so what difference would it make? No matter where he was in an emergency he could be there in half a day. The good life was a distant past, the new life exasperating and wearisome. If it were only a bad dream he lamented.

What if Sander never returns the calls he wondered. Should he stay put until he heard from him? Had something unimaginable happened? A phone call to the airline settled the issue. He'd leave on the first flight out the next evening unless he heard from Sander. There was no call.

In mid flight Theo felt the panic attack come on fast and hard, laser beams and lightening bolts bombarding the inside of his eyelids. The journey suddenly became overwhelming and for the first time, painful. Rent a car and simply drive to the town hall and everything would be settled he could not convince himself. Theo lifted the sweater inside his carryon bag making certain the child size flight jacket was not left home.

He cursed the jacket, too small to be Hess' so why was it aboard the aircraft and who did it belong to?

Upon landing he experienced something he'd never felt before. The distance from Noah could have been the distance from the moon. He couldn't shake the blues and if they got any worse he'd rush back to the airport and get home as quickly as possible he decided.

If only Sander had called back saying he was alright he rued. Why hadn't he called back? Was he still living in the town hall tending to his town duties or had he found new quarters? Hardly recognizing the towns he'd passed through once with Noah it felt as if he'd never been there.

Welcome to Eaglesham he said aloud. Driving into the town center he spied the town hall and further down the old inn. Dashing up the old steps to the heavy oaken doors he was suddenly dismayed, the doors locked. Pounding on the door was fruitless, stopping only after an elderly woman passing said if the door was locked nobody was in.

"The town hall isn't open on Sunday" she announced knowingly. The frustration level was in the mortal danger zone and he cursed. If there ever a final last straw it was the moment his once controllable anger bubbled to the surface, a step deeper into the void before him. Watching the woman walk away he realized she was the only one out and about. Getting back into his rental Theo took the now familiar road to the McCann homestead in the country.

Stopping at the location where he and Noah first parked their bikes, he peered over the hedge rows observing the scattered boulders.

It took a few moments before he assumed he'd made a wrong turn. Something wasn't quite right but he couldn't put his finger on it just yet no matter how hard he stared. Then it hit him like a clap of thunder on a clear day. The once standing McCann homestead was simply gone. Slapping the steering wheel harder and harder he cursed his stupidity, making a wrong turn and getting lost. The only logical answer was he'd stopped the car too soon, overlooking a different settlement he hadn't seen before. Back on the road the narrow lane soon grew quite steep and gravely, darkened by the encroaching woods. Could I have taken the wrong fork he wondered? It seemed impossible but he guessed he had. Did I turn onto Patience and not take the right fork? Was I on Hope leading to another ancient settlement?

Turning around and stopping once again at the familiar overlook he peered deep into the valley expecting to see the sole stone house standing among the ruins. It simply was not there. There could be only one explanation he whined. He'd lost his mind.

Staring at the stones so fixedly his eyes blurred, he shouted to the heavens where am I? Three weeks had passed since he'd said farewell to Sander so had something unimaginable happen during that time? It was completely incomprehensible. Was Sander holed up once again in his tiny office in the town hall? Had the Brits caught him living there? Had Sander found another home?

He sat atop one large boulder certain it came from Sander's old homestead. It was different than the other scattered and broken stones, coated with black most likely soot from recent peat fires. No other stones in the valley were blackened, too much weathering he knew.

He picked through rubble for any evidence of the old McCann homestead finding nothing, as if vultures had picked the place clean. Not a peat of brick, stick of furniture, old toys and books or kitchen utensils could be found. Theo was entirely certain it was once the McCann farm. Not far from where the house once rested hundred of broken shards spotted with sooty black streaks were scattered.

Beating himself up at the absurdity of his life he hoped he'd finally reached bottom. It can't get any worse he prayed. The emptiness in the valley was something he could identify with, feeling as if he were all alone in the world. He urged himself to pull it together in order to drive safely back into town to find answers. Perhaps Franz the innkeeper might help him understand what he could not comprehend. Sadly he knew he'd have to wait until Monday when the town hall opened to find Sander.

Sunday, Sunday, Sunday cried in desperation, the town entirely closed up, the only unlocked door in the entire village the entrance to the old inn. Franz greeted him with a smile and a questioning look in his eyes. "Greta, look who the cat just dragged in."

Feeling the lost soul Theo knew it would be preposterous to explain his sudden reappearance. He did let on he had some unfinished business with his great uncle, leaving Noah home.

Wondering if the couple had seen Sander recently he still didn't ask, suspecting it would lead to a conversation he wished to avoid. The greeting was warm and cordial which lifted his spirit's a bit. Franz asked if he'd like his old room and he replied no. The thought of being there without Noah would be unbearable, saying a smaller room would be better.

Greta offered a welcoming drink on the house but knowing it would lead to small talk he declined the generous offer.

"No dinner service tonight" she offered "but I can make you a sandwich if you'd like." The offer was heartfelt, a simple kindness making his eyes moisten. It seemed as if everything was making him teary these days he understood. The salad sandwich consisted of lettuce, tomato, too much mayonnaise and a slice of cheese on brown bread. His growling stomach at the sight of food made for much laughter, admitting he'd not eaten anything all day.

One thing he didn't hesitate asking was what time the old town hall opened in the morning. Greta said she'd ask Franz because she wasn't certain. She was soon at his door with an answer, accompanied by an armful of peat for the fireplace. "Anytime after ten you should find someone in the town hall, either Mrs. Tavish or your uncle. No one really knows for certain when the town hall might open because we're a very tiny village with few needs.

The unheated room definitely needed peat for light and warmth. The smell of dried peat burning created an instant soothing effect, a treasure he'd missed while home. The fire as it had in the many hours in Sander's home created peace, almost guaranteeing to quiet an overactive mind. The underlying fear melted as the room warmed, wondering if he could fall asleep under a heavy comforter for days.

In the morning Greta prepared a breakfast fit for royalty, enough to feed an army Theo joked. Franz stopped by the table in the tiny breakfast nook asking if Theo might enjoy some company. Desperate to be alone until he was certain Sander was okay he had to say yes to the kindly innkeeper.

Franz could be sixty five or seventy he guessed, a weathered tawny face with deep blue eyes visible under his bushy white eyebrows. "Tell me Franz, how long have you and Greta owned the inn? Were you born here?"

"Going on nearly thirty years believe it or not. We were living in Glasgow where we're both originally from. On one extended holiday we came to this area to trek and camp for a couple of weeks. One of the trails we followed led to the village of Eaglesham, Greta and I tired and thirsty. It was either fate or simply just the way the trail meandered that brought us here that day. I remember it well because something dreadful happened while ambling triumphantly into the town square like a conquering hero. On one of the poorly maintained sidewalks I tripped and fell, discovering later I'd broken my ankle. Limping painfully toward the only open door on the plaza, it just happened to be a rundown village inn, this one. I can't begin to describe the terrible disrepair but to me in my time of need it was an oasis. It would do because I needed to find a doctor and had to stay off my feet.

"For a few pounds a night we overlooked the nastiness and squalor, Greta nursing me until she couldn't stand my grumpiness any longer. She'd been told about some easy walking trails nearby and with me not needing a full time nurse anymore she went out exploring on her own. The trails kept her outside the daylight hours, me just resting my foot and reading. As you might imagine as the only guest I got to know the innkeeper well, a man by the name of McGregor.

"Lots of small talk at first until one day I asked about the history of the inn. It must have been quite charming once I sensed, still homey though even in disrepair. McGregor never talked about the building's condition but he did say it was on it's last legs. Six or seven days later he came to my room, a sullen look on his face with bad news. I'd have to find another place to rehab because the bank was taking his place due to his inability to pay the mortgage. The real kicker was, the building was going to be condemned. In those days there were no other lodgings in Eaglesham, several though in far off villages.

"I learned much about McGregor during our last days, hobbling downstairs to spend a few pleasant hours playing chess. I'd grown rather fond of the place but don't ask me why. It exuded a certain charm making me want to stay forever. McGregor talked about the lack of tourists and how it became more and more impossible to keep the place up. I told him I wished I could lend him money to hang on a bit longer but he insisted he was getting out of the innkeeper business for good, not wanting to leave debt behind.

"That night a crazy thought wouldn't let go of me. Greta and I knew a bit about the hotel business, managing a small tourist hotel in Glasgow for a few years. When the work was slow we'd tell each other one day we'd own our own small inn. Coincidence, fate or dumb luck breaking an ankle led us here so I figured, why not make an offer.

"During the last breakfast together I asked McGregor if he had any interested in selling the inn, that was if someone offered a fair price. Remember this was a long time ago and the cost of an old rundown inn was very respectable. Asking what he might sell it for well, as the saying goes the price was right and a few minutes later we shook hands and hobbled over to the bank.

"McGregor got enough money to repay the bank allowing he and his wife to move back to Glasgow. I remember the exact date and time we signed the papers. It was June 29, 1955 and to honor that special day every year I invite all the townsfolk here for a banquet. I've continued that tradition for many years."

It was well past ten in the morning and the town hall was on Theo's mind. He thanked Franz for his hospitality but had to leave to see Sander.

The town plaza as usual was empty, a few women in dull gray aprons sweeping sidewalks with hungry stray dogs following. Peeking in the stained glass window of the town hall Theo thought it much too dark and probably not open yet. The old iron door knob surprisingly turned, buoying his spirits. Stepping inside he was temporarily blinded going from the bright sunlight into darkness. Theo had the odd feeling he'd just walked into another century.

Somewhere beyond the tiny entry he heard the voice of a woman asking him if she might help him. Theo asked if she were Mrs. Tavish. Her reply was an intimidating stare, eying him long and carefully. "How would a complete stranger know my name" she asked?

Theo said his name, emphasizing McCann. An apology was needed he understood in order to get in the woman's good graces, recalling his rude phone calls. Apologizing he said he was the person who'd called a number of times trying to get in touch with Mr. Sander McCann.

"A number of times?"

Walking to the small welcoming desk Theo got down to business, "Is Mr. McCann alright?" Eyeing the door behind the desk to Sander's unofficial home he wondered if he should just walk past and knock on the door.

"Come outside with me for a minute" she whispered. The way the words were spoken portended something bad might have happened.

Sitting on the front steps observing shop owners opening their small businesses, they sat for a while in an uncomfortable silence.

"Why did you sound so desperate on the phone" she asked? "By the way I'm one of the privileged few allowed to call him by his first name. I assure you I passed each and every message along."

Feelings of guilt surfaced remembering how very ungracious he was on the phone. "Please tell me Mrs. Tavish, has something happened to my uncle?"

"I'll get straight to the point Mr. McCann. A few days before your first call everyone in the village heard a very loud explosion just west of here, certainly not thunder. Several townspeople took to their bicycles and peddled off to investigate. They followed a plume of black smoke drifting skyward from somewhere near Patience Lane but the men never made it. Soldiers set up a road block declaring the road closed until further notice. No reason was given nor was there any hint to what the explosion was. The men returned with the news of being stopped, speculation running rampant as you might imagine.

"Hours passed and Sander eventually appeared, walking slowly and looking totally despondent. I ran to greet him asking about the explosion. He said not one word, continuing up the town hall steps into his tiny office, the door locked behind him and he remained there to this day.

"I shooed everyone out of the building, locked the front door and proceeded to knock on Mr. McCann's door. There was no response which was terribly unsettling and unexplainable. Going home hours later nervous and confused I eventually returned bringing Sander dinner. I'd made salmon croquettes his favorite. I shouted through the door we were all very worried about him but alas no response. I hate to admit this but I worried he'd done something to hurt himself.

"I worked the front desk the next two days, taking your phone calls and tending to business. Believe me I relayed every message through that closed door, leaving a food tray on the floor before I left in the afternoon. In the morning the empty tray was there, a great relief.

"On your ninth or tenth call I wrote down your exact words again, sliding the note under the door. I'd wait for a moment or two but the door never opened. Gathering my things to lock up and leave a few days ago I mercifully heard his voice. He came out looking around as if he didn't recognize his surroundings. He asked me to step into his office.

"I'm certain it's okay to tell you this being kin and all but maybe you could not mention our conversation when you see him. Sander does things on own schedule but I'm sure he'll tell you the entire story. Act as if you're hearing it for the first time please.

"Not sure if you knew but he'd actually moved out of his homestead many years ago, long before I worked here. He created a little home for himself in the storeroom behind my desk. One evening before closing time, possibly six months after I began working he said it was time to get something off his chest. He told me a very sad tale which troubled me greatly. The property and his home didn't belong to him anymore he said, owned now by British authorities. That seemed quite odd because the British had no claim on our land but I never doubted his words. With great wretchedness he said he'd been ordered out of his home many years earlier, told to pack up his belongings and never return. I hope that explosion we heard had nothing to do with his going back to the old homestead to live. He always hinted he'd planned on opening the homestead one day.

"When you showed up with your son he was very skeptical of strangers until you told him you were a descendent of the McCann's of Eaglesham. He told me it took a little time reconciling you were actually American kin, not British authority. I can tell you from the little Sander told me about you that your appearance was a good omen meaning it was the right time to move back into the old McCann homestead. The moment he decided to move home I thought he looked better and happier than I'd ever seen. He was so animated and I attribute that to you.

"Well sir as I said, something happened five days ago, the explosion and the smoke rattling the village and all. Hours later Sander walked into town looking as if he'd been dragged under a truck. From the few words he spoke only to me, he whispered the British authorities must have learned he'd relocated back to his home. He knew he was trespassing and the property off limits but the indignation and outright anger had finally come to a boiling point. He was going to defy them. I have no idea what exploded because Sander refused to talk about it. Too painful I guess.

"If you'll take some advice from someone who knows Sander better than anyone else in the village here it goes. Go knock on his door and let him know you're here because I think the sound of your voice will get him out of his cocoon. If Sander asks about me, tell him it was a very slow day and I needed to do a bit of marketing. Tell him that I also let you in.

He could have hugged Mrs. Tavish. Theo apologized again for being an ass, making them both smile.

Knocking gently at first then with authority, he said it's me Theo, returning to Scotland to finish some work we need to do.

Chapter Twenty Two

The sound of feet shuffling followed by the door slowly opening, the two eying each other with curious stares. Sander appeared to have aged ten years in the short time he was away Theo thought. Life had not been good. Hugging his thin body he scolded Sander for not taking better care of himself.

"Sander what ever happened I want you to know I'll do everything in my power to help and that's the reason I'm here so my first question is, why are you living here and what happened while I was away? Can you explain what happened at the homestead?

Sander stared off into space. Not a good sign Theo rued.

"Where's the boy" he whispered?

"Not to worry" Theo said assuredly. "He's home getting the help he desperately needs." Sander nodded, standing aside allowing Theo to enter.

Settling uneasily into the oversized old chairs Theo was certain something was terribly wrong. A deliberate and emotionally filled Sander explained.

"Seven days ago several military vehicles drove through the village right up to my front door outside of town. Some men were in military uniforms, others wearing civilian clothing. One of the men shouted orders from a seat atop one of the vehicles directing his men to search the property and my home. I was ordered out but first I ducked into dark corner saying I needed a jacket which was no lie. I stuffed the child sized jacket under my coat double timing to the post office where I mailed it to you, the only safe place I reasoned. I was afraid the men would find it because they were very thorough. I guess it was quite a surprise when the package showed up at your place.

"I'm pretty certain why my house was destroyed and I'll get to that in a moment. Some very odd things have happened here and I sense Rudolf Hess' death had everything to do with it.

"If you remember forty years ago I was ordered out of my home, warned to stay away or face dire consequences. I had little more than a day to leave the property, centuries of McCann life ending in moments. Even then I always thought when the Hess story became old news I'd be able to return. Constantly on edge those hectic day there were still veiled threats.

"They came again, not the same soldiers but for the same purpose to evict me knowing it had to do with the death of Rudolf Hess. None of my questions were answered, as if they were all deaf. I think the underlying reason the authorities in Scotland wanted the home destroyed was so it wouldn't turn into a neo-Nazi shrine, like Spandau Prison and his grave site and a few other Nazi places.

"If you remember my saying Horn also known as Hess did a thorough search of the entire area around the crash scene, most likely for something that could have been thrown from the wreckage. What he was looking for I knew was not found, nor was it found by the soldiers. Every square inch of my homestead was gone through with a fine toothed comb. That was a long time ago but some days it feels like yesterday. So why did the authorities return to Eaglesham this time? How did they know I'd moved back into the homestead? I believe I just got caught up in their devious plan to erase all evidence of Hess' presence on this earth.

"Just like that day in May of 1941 I gathered my belongings again. This time I was given only until six the next morning to get out.

127

"At six sharp the next day a soldier walked into my house telling me it was time, holding the door open for emphasis. I had no idea what would happen next, nor did the soldiers seem to be interested in what was happening to me. Several uniformed men poked through the cartons I'd packed saying they'd be driven to the town hall. It was against military law I was told allowing civilians to ride in military vehicles. I dragged my sorry ass back to town on foot.

"I was probably a mile down the road, half in a daze when I heard a loud explosion knowing immediately what it was. My heart broke.

"I knew all the materials from the demolished Spandau prison had been ground into powder and dispersed in the North Sea. Was that the fate of my home? The British kept one set of prison keys, everything else methodically disposed in secret. I came to believe any and all traces of Hess' existence on this earth were going to disappear."

Theo's gut was a tangle of pains and anger drawn sadly into Sander's wretchedness. "Where do we go from here Sander" Theo asked, "I'm here for you."

"Theo you can do me a huge favor, something I've been thinking about for several days and nights. By the way you're certainly a sight for sorrowful eyes and truthfully I never expected to see you again because of Noah's issues and all. Forgive me for not asking about Noah but I seem to be caught up in myself.

"There's something I have to do as soon as possible for the people of this village and I'll need your help. I'm not as agile as I once was so here's my idea. I'd like you to go to the back of the entry hall where you'll find a door. Open it and you'll see a precarious set of steep stairs leading up to the old bell tower. Be extremely careful because I don't know what shape the metal and wooden steps are in. When you get to the top landing you'll find a platform to stand on. Look straight up and you'll see a chain. The chain's attached to the large bell given to the village in 1558. It has not been rung since the day the Great War ended in 1919. Be careful because I don't know how fragile the area is.

"The older townspeople know the large bell rings only if something extraordinary or momentous has occurred. It's a call for the townspeople to gather to be informed about something that might affect them. I believe it's the right time to share the Hess saga with these people and his connection to Eaglesham. Given how I've been treated by the British authorities I don't give a damn for them or their threats. I owe my friends a long overdue explanation so can you try to ring that bell for me?"

"Are you sure you want to involve the people of the village in the Hess chronicle? What would they gain from it?"

"I think my friends deserve to know the true story. Rumors and cover ups have always been rife, regretfully most of it misinformation or half truths. Something quite extraordinary occurred here and I'd like them to learn about it because the loud explosion has the village abuzz. I used to laugh over an occasional pint at the inn when someone might ask if a flying saucer landed on my property. I need to do this because they deserve to know."

Without questioning Sander's decision Theo found the doorway and the darkened stairs leading to the bell tower. With no light it was a methodical climb up the steep incline, heart pounding not because of exertion but because of what Sander was about to do.

Feeing for the chain in the dark proved fruitless until Theo literally walked into it. With both hands tightly wrapped around the thick rusted chain he tugged but nothing happened. The chain he assumed was corroded by moisture over the centuries, frozen and useless. Reaching higher up on the chain he took a firmer grip, pulling himself off the floor rising higher, his feet no longer touching.

Gravity took over but the chain still couldn't make the large bell toll. Twisting and pulling as hard as could the chain began to loosen a bit. Fearing more tension might drop the heavy bell on top of him and about to abandon the effort, to his great surprise the sound of tolling began, a muted sound but it worked.

One final pull created a great whirring noise as hundreds of chimney birds fled the commotion, their wings sounding like thunder. Pulling down once again the strike was forceful enough to create a thunderous clap, it's sound deafening inside the hollow tower. Keeping up the effort he began to hear the sound of voices far below, the first to arrive in the great hall. The task completed Theo made his way down the narrow corridor to the main floor. His eyes couldn't immediately adjust to the bright light but when they did he saw the large entry hall filled with town's people.

Sander stood atop the reception desk, a most serious and determined look waiting for quiet. "I need to tell you a story about something that's affected my life for more than forty years and now, something that might impact your lives."

Seeing Theo he motioned to get up onto the desk with him. In a firm unwavering voice Sander began to relive all that had been pent up and locked inside.

Chapter Twenty Three

"I thank you all for coming here and after I explain why you've been summoned, you'll understand a most extraordinary event that took place here in Eaglesham nearly fifty two years ago. It continues to have a stranglehold on my life and possibly, soon to involve some of you. Many in this room have lived here all their lives but old timer or newcomer you are all deeply imbedded in our tiny close knit community. On May 11, 1941 something quite extraordinary happened here in Eaglesham village, something that possibly had a great impact on the war waging across the continent.

"On May 11th I was working the land around the McCann homestead when my ears picked up a strange sound. Looking up I witnessed a plane spiraling out of control, hurtling toward the earth not far from where I stood. In a nightmarish scenario the plane smashed into pieces, parts falling from the sky for minutes like rain. Looking in the direction of the sky where I'd first noticed the noise I saw a billowing white parachute and what appeared to be someone slumped in a harness. I assumed it was the pilot, motionless when he landed hard, unable to tell if the airman were dead or alive.

"I ran toward him believing he was most likely an RAF pilot on a training mission. Observing him moving his arms and legs was heartwarming because I didn't believe he could have survived.

"Spying me the pilot spoke in halting English, telling me his name was Albert Horn. I wasn't certain who was more stunned, the wayward pilot or me while he worked desperately to disentangle himself from the harness. I could tell by his movements he seemed quite fragile but appeared no worse for what he'd been through. The destroyed aircraft was smoldering but not on fire. He claimed to have run out of fuel necessitating bailing out. Some of you probably remember the classes we took in the late thirties and early forties teaching us how to identify German aircraft. That education came in handy because I discovered it was not an RAF aircraft, but a destroyed German Messerschmitt. The airman pulled himself to his feet tottering like a new born calf. I was convinced he was not RAF, the German lettering on the flight suit and the wreckage convincing me.

"The airman asked me to help him search the crash site, saying something extremely valuable was probably still inside the wreck. There was great urgency in his voice, almost fanatical. It was quite chilly and after thirty minutes of kicking parts aside I invited him into my home to warm by the fire.

"When his color came back he looked totally exhausted, saying his plan was to land safely on the Duke of Hamilton's estate. He rued the fact he'd ran out of fuel before he could land, cursing himself. When I told him he was only twenty kilometers from the estate he shook his head, mumbling the words so close.

"Might I give him a ride in my horse carriage to the Duke's estate he asked, saying there was something extremely important he needed to discuss. I replied I didn't own a horse and carriage but there were walking trails in the woods leading to the Duke's estate, probably eight or ten hours walking time. That was just about the amount of daylight left so I told him he'd better be off right away if he wanted to make it by nightfall. The airman asked me to accompany him for fear of getting lost. Time was critical and why I agreed I honestly don't remember.

"We started out but not five hundred meters away a large helicopter circled overhead, eventually landing in a clearing some distance in front of us. Two soldiers, definitely RAF jumped out of the helicopter running toward us. The noise from the rotors made it hard to hear so I was not privy to their conversation. The RAF men spoke with Horn for several minutes, then took him by his arms pulling him toward the helicopter. I started to follow but one of the soldiers turned and approached me. I was told in no uncertain terms I was to return to my home and wait there. Do not speak a word of what happened here to anyone I was warned. The helicopter flew away with Horn aboard, watching from my doorstep until it disappeared.

"Friends and neighbors I was threatened never to relate what I'd seen and heard. I could not share what happened, threatened with dire consequences. I'm sorry I've waited so long to share this with you but I do so now because our village might become a haven for neo-Nazis. You see, the airman's real name was Rudolf Hess, the Nazi who died several weeks ago in West Germany." The loud audible gasp echoed around the room.

"The man who fell from the sky, the man I helped turned out not to be Albert Horn but a high ranking Nazi official, the infamous Nazi."

In time so many voices shouted out it sounded like an engine being revved. A man not five feet from Sander shouted it was no secret. "Everyone in Scotland was aware Hess parachuted into an unknown place nearby, supposedly on a secret mission. I don't believe any of us had a clue that it was here in Eaglesham though."

When the voices quieted Sander continued.

"Rudolf Hess fell to earth not far from this building, purportedly on a mission of peace. Mere weeks after Hess's flight Hitler turned his forces east with a massive invasion of the Soviet Union. The history of World War Two highlights Hess' flight because it was one of the war's strangest incidents. Much information about Hess' flight has not been made public but due to his recent death the world is getting quite an education. Rudolf Hess, the last remaining Nazi prisoner in Spandau Prison died at the age of ninety-three a few weeks ago.

"The loud explosion you heard was the destruction of my home, a place where generations of McCann's lived and worked. I believe it was destroyed so it would not become a neo-Nazi pilgrimage site.

"The day the British discovered Rudolf Hess crashed onto a Scottish farm life changed dramatically for me. When the world was informed Hess was a prisoner of war held by the British, false information and rumors spread like wildfire. If you haven't heard this one, one rumor says it was not Hess who flew here but a body double. His personal journey remains a mystery and a state secret.

"What happened during the days after the airman fell from the sky onto my property? To my absolute astonishment I was visited by the indomitable Sir Winston Churchill, appearing at my doorstep to question me. Demanding to know what the airman and I discussed you can imagine I was in a total state of confusion. My home was torn apart by soldiers, searched as if they knew something had been left behind or hidden. They did however overlook one very important article and I will tell you about that shortly.

"None of you are in danger of having your homes searched or blown up by British authorities, but you might see strangers in and about the village. We who live in Eaglesham are inexplicably attached to the Hess saga and so the mystery continues.

"I'll be staying in the town hall in my little apartment taking care of village business as usual. This gentleman next to me is my great nephew Theo McCann, an American staying at the inn for a short visit. I've asked for his help while I attempt to find new living quarters. I'll keep you informed about anything that might arise, hopefully nothing dramatic. You are not in danger but I would ask you to keep an eye out for strangers. Hess in life stirred many followers to plunge into the depths of hell with him, and the sons and daughters of those individuals carry on his cause. Bless you all for coming here to listen to an old windbag. I thought it important."

The audience turned deathly quiet until someone yelled, "You didn't tell us anything we didn't know but you've convinced me and others you certainly are the town windbag. By the way that's why we love you. They might have destroyed your home but we've got your back."

The townsfolk left abuzz on the way to their homes, many wondering aloud if all was really safe to walk the streets of Eaglesham.

CHAPTER TWENTY FOUR

Sander suggested not returning to the inn until most of the town's people were safely home. "If they see you they'll have a hell of a lot of questions, most you won't have answers for. Come on in the backroom and I'll put some real coffee on, knowing you Americans prefer it to tea."

Sitting by the peat fire Sander said he was pleased he could be open and honest with the townsfolk. "You know Theo, if word ever gets out to the outside world that Hess landed in this village it could easily be turned into a shrine. My hope is all the people of this village gets on with their lives but remaining a bit cautious about strangers." The address was emotional Theo added but filled with assurances.

Sander threw a few new peat bricks into the fire declaring "whatever ails you, you can always find momentary peace beside a good peat fire. I feel as if a huge weight was taken off my aching shoulders, finally able to look my neighbors in the eye and be open."

Sitting close to the fire with fresh coffee and home baked scones Theo felt relaxed, his thoughts turning to Noah. Neither man said much for a long time until Sander suggested it was a good time to walk back to the inn. "I nearly forgot asking did you receive the package with the flight jacket inside?"

Nodding, Theo left saying he'd be back in the morning.

He asked if he might use the inn's phone to make a long distance call to America, assuring he'd pay for it. Despite the drama of the later afternoon and early evening Noah was never far from his thoughts. If there were problems he understood he could be in Glasgow in an hour and on a morning flight home the next day. There were no messages at the inn, a sign all was most likely well at the institute.

Holding off on the call until morning was an easy decision. He badly needed sleep. Franz unfortunately followed him to his room asking what was happening at the town hall.

"I'll fill you in tomorrow morning if you don't mind." Franz merely shrugged his shoulders and walked away.

After an hour of tossing he could wait no longer, needing to make a decisive phone call. When a woman answered at the institute he asked to speak with Dr. Ark. His request was met with laughter, a reaction that did not sit well.

"If she's busy would you please give her a message then?" His second request was met with more laughter, sounding awfully fake he suspected.

"Sir I can't get Dr. Ark on the phone because only the night crew is working at this hour. Are you aware there are no therapists here at this hour? It's three in the morning so is this an emergency?"

Despite being three thousand miles away Theo felt foolish, embarrassed at his gaffe. Stammering an apology he sheepishly begged her to forget the call and no, it was not an emergency.

It had been some time since he'd slept well, often waking with a start discovering Noah was not sleeping by his side. He couldn't remember the last time he'd eaten anything but the salad sandwich or the last time he slept well but he was neither tired or hungry. Theo's stomach felt like a fully loaded washing machine, churning his life apart.

He searched the room for a hiding place for the flight jacket and when he found it he was able to fall into a deep sleep. In the morning he shared the breakfast table with Franz and Greta, offering a modified account of the previous evening's events. Greta said she hoped Sander was alright. Franz said nothing but Theo noticed a troubled look on his face.

Arriving at Sander's unofficial home he found it littered with what was salvaged from the old homestead. The first order of business after straightening things up and getting a fire going was what is to be done with the flight jacket, the only physical reminder of a mystery that had few answers.

"Theo why don't we kick this Hess thing around and see where it goes. I'd also appreciate if you'd catch me up on some things you might have learned at home."

"Actually I did some searching into Hess' life although half heartedly I admit. It was not engaging because you were not by my side. Like you I discovered there are many gray areas in his life, both before and after his flight. Thanks to you I already knew the basics of the Hess' story so I used the time looking for anything I might find that was either forgotten or overlooked. Sadly nothing new to report and for your information, I could not find the slightest hint there might have been a passenger on board. There were no rumors, no sensational stories in the scandal papers, no nothing. Is it possible Hess didn't know he had a passenger aboard, possibly a stowaway fleeing the chaos in Germany? Maybe somehow he wasn't aware someone snuck into his aircraft. One old news article highlighted the fact the British felt certain something important could still be buried near where the destroyed aircraft fell. From your personal encounter you probably already knew this but I'll go over a few things I found. He came with a set of maps of England and North-western Europe, A German Lugar pistol allegedly fully loaded, British pounds, fake identity cards, a camera, binoculars and pills later identified as strychnine. The aircraft didn't go up in flames so what was recovered in the wreckage was most likely gone through with the proverbial comb. It's possible there were other items brought along but we'll never know."

"The British troops methodically searched Theo and I know because I was standing less than a hundred feet away. They didn't find the flight jacket for certain thanks to my rash and possibly idiot decision to stash it where it couldn't be found. If there was a passenger it's possible he might have been thrown far from the wreckage, injured but alive. That's pure speculation however and might be the furthest thing from reality. To this day I still swear I saw only one parachute. If there had been a second it's possible it might have drifted out of my sight behind the woods. Certain portions of Hess' interrogation were released over the years and in one Hess related he'd blacked out the moment he bailed from the plane. From my personal vantage point he was intently looking for something in the wreckage. Maybe it was the small fight jacket or the broken body of a child, or maybe something personal."

"Two extra fuel tanks were recovered" Theo added. "Not sure if you knew but when Hess was asked why they'd been added he said he wanted to see if they could be used to mine British ports. Apparently several photos were found on his body of the Duke of Hamilton's estate as well as an old photograph showing the Duke and Hess together at the 1936 Berlin Olympics. Shall I go on?"

Sander nodded.

"If there is a case to be built for a passenger here's something I found interesting. The Germans were excellent record keepers as the world later discovered. When the Allied forces liberated Germany thousands of ledger books were recovered, a few containing receipts for goods purchased by Nazi party members. Many receipts came from the clothier Schwarz Taylor, a shop frequented by Nazi officials in Munich. One individual receipt detailed purchases made by one Rudolf Hess, ordering not one but two blue-grey flight jackets, different sizes for three hundred marks total. As an aside the Luftwaffe uniform Hess actually wore on the flight remained his personal property, kept by his side in his prison cell at Spandau until his death a few weeks ago. The other jacket? That one was seemingly given to you. Why? Was it simply a gesture of thanks or was there a sinister reason?

"It's a mystery wrapped inside a mystery and enigma inside another enigma Sander. I brought along a Washington DC newspaper obituary written about Hess because it was the most straightforward. It claims the only worldly possession Hess left behind in the prison after his death was his beloved flight jacket, to be given to Hess' adult son. Incredibly it was stolen before it could be transferred, possibly by a guard at Spandau Prison.

"Since Hess' death a few rather benign files have been released to the public. Why now? I believe it was the British throwing crumbs to the public so it could be said the file is now officially closed. There's a lot more to Hess than they're letting on and I'd bet money on that.

"Theo I kept few articles printed in local papers back in 1941, somewhere in all this mess. If I recall one details a rendezvous with a man he considered his mentor. His name was Albrecht Haushofer. When I attempted to investigate who this man was I discovered the Gestapo had murdered him near the end of the war.

"Somewhere in my files are a few grainy pictures I received from a detective friend. The friend took the photos the day of the flight from Augsburg, Germany. There's a leather satchel in his grasp in the photo. According to a reporter on the scene Hess was asked what was in the bag but there was no response.

"In another cruel twist of fate Sander I read that Hess' personal files had been locked securely in his office, later removed by Martin Bormann, an aide to Hitler. He had sole charge of them until the day his office was searched by marauding Russian solders after the war. The papers were taken by the Russians but were not introduced into evidence against Hess at the trials. When it was later announced the Russians would publish those papers, they were stolen from the extremely secure Palace of Justice in Nuremberg. This whole Hess saga is just one gigantic mystery.

"Some of Hess' personal papers Theo will be released to the public in the coming months as reported by the BBC. I'm not certain if it's the British or the Germans trying to appease those like you who have remaining doubts about Hess' mission. Many transcripts and documents are still tightly sealed, the reason if they were released they would cause substantive distress to Hess' relatives.

"Only five people are alive today privy to Hess' personal files and the interrogation notes written by Churchill and others. I very seriously doubt they'll ever be released. Speculation runs wild in third rate newspapers, including the theory Hess was actually lured to Britain by elements of British intelligence.

"The Germans steadfastly put forth the notion Hess was stark raving mad, a psychopath, end of story. The opportunity to examine Hess after his capture would certainly have given Britain the ability to make sense of what forces drove the Nazis. There has to be notes somewhere on the interrogations in someone's locked files but they might as well be lost. Hess remained defiant until his last breath, furious he was considered a common prisoner and not treated as a peace envoy. In death more information about Hess and his mission will undoubtedly be released but many critical pieces are forever bound under tight British scrutiny. Why nearly fifty years after the end of the war is it necessary to keep secrets? There must be some very damaging information out there and perhaps the world will never know."

CHAPTER TWENTY FIVE

"We can certainly connect the child's jacket to Hess because it went directly from his hands into mine" Sander said. "Was it a gift for the Duke or was there really a passenger? Is there any real significance to it" Sander said ruefully? "The answers if there are any are not going to be discovered anytime soon.

"Theo the Duke was well known to neighbors although he kept to himself. Some investigating by me proved he was childless, living on his large estate with wife and servants. For that reason I suspect the jacket was not meant as a gift for him. I never spoke with the Duke personally but I spied him once or twice during fox hunting season when he came onto my property. A grand sight to see."

"What else did you learn about Mr. Hess" Sander asked?

"The reality the Germans moved very quickly to dissociate Hess from the regime when his flight became public knowledge. A Nazi party spokesperson declared Hess suffered from a mental disturbance with hallucinations, therefore not at all credible. For good or bad everything released to the public omits any reference to the idea a passenger might have been brought along. Did Hitler know of Hess' undertaking or was he completely blindsided? Some pretty damning evidence suggests it was Hitler's idea. Years ago the Russians announced they possessed a letter stored in their State Archives suggesting Hitler was a partner in Hess' mission. Regretfully that note will never be seen.

"Evidence does illustrate a fact the mission was undertaken to promote a military alliance between England and Germany against the Soviet Union. British intelligence services might even have been in touch with Hess, possibly duping him into the flight as crazy as that sounds. As to where this all goes the sad reality is we're never going to see much of that information. Sander, the jacket is a dead end. The Nazi Albert Speer insisted it was Hess' idea entirely, claiming the mission was created in a dream Hess claimed to have had involving supernatural forces. Speer and Hess were both incarcerated at Spandau so it's possible they might have shared secrets. Speer died some years ago and Hess finally joined him

"Unfortunately the riddle about the second jacket cannot be solved by you or me. Some important documents might have been destroyed over time, stashed away or lost. Someone high up probably has all the answers though, charged with keeping a tight lid on them. After Hess' death Reuters news service attempted to get hold of many files but were told they were still classified."

"Got anything else?"

"An American auction house once offered unopened papers the British once marked top secret regarding Hess, bought up by an anonymous buyer. It was thought they contained nearly three hundred pages written by him during his wartime captivity. He brought them to the major war crime tribunal but guess what? They disappeared.

"Who got their hands on them and why? Rumor has it a wealthy German bought them but shortly after he and the papers disappeared.

"That's all very interesting Sander but none of it gets you any closer to discovering any information about the child's jacket."

"Theo during an inquiry into Hess's affairs held in Glasgow in the 1950's by so called experts, the committee attempted to expose much of what the world was denied. During the hearings open to the public by the way it was revealed Hess was briefly interrogated by Scottish officials before British intelligence stepped in. Several notable sources said the commission was on the trail of the real truth about the mission but before it could be finalized, British intelligence disbanded the committee."

"Sander what have you read or heard about Hitler knowing about Hess' secret plan and possibly had him murdered? That's where the rumors an imposter was sent in his place arose from. Some suppositions offer different interpretations of the Hess story including one fascinating declassified note stating that after a routine physical done by doctors before the Nuremburg trial, there were certain unexplainable issues. The doctor's stated Hess didn't bear any scars he'd suffered in World War One. The conclusion? Hess did not make that flight. British engineers also concluded no matter how many extra fuel tanks Hess attached to his plane, the ME110 would not have the fuel capacity to make a direct flight to Scotland. If that were true he refueled someplace, possibly with the help of the British. So many unexplained ingredients in this mystery."

"Sander I spent a few evenings listening to BBC news at home in the evenings and there was considerable commentary about Hess' funeral. The original plan it seems was to bury Hess in the family plot but that soon became a huge miscalculation. After his internment the grave was overrun with neo-Nazis paying tribute. Days later his body was secretly removed from the grave site and cremated, his ashes scattered at sea in order to stop neo-Nazi's from visiting his final resting place. The family had the last say when and where the ashes would be scattered."

"Sander, are you concerned about Eaglesham becoming a neo-Nazi shrine? Some recent articles relating to Hess describe skinheads and far right extremists gathering in large numbers at sites associated with top Nazi officials. With Hess' death is it possible even the small village Eaglesham might be over run by some disreputable people. I saved this article from the Times published a few days after the Nuremburg tribunal ended. It's one of the few things I found in Hess' own words.

'My coming to England in that way was so unusual nobody will easily understand. I was confronted by a very hard decision. I do not think I could have arrived at my final destination unless I kept before me the vision of an endless line of children's coffins with weeping mothers about. Another vision was a line of coffins with mothers mourning children.'

"There are hundreds of other quirks about Hess' life and death Sander but I don't think anything of importance will be released anytime soon. The world believes the last footnotes in Hess' history have been written. If you consider all rumors, the innuendos, the scandals and unproven and proven theories attributed to Hess, the search for the owner of this jacket would seem impossible.

"I hope that puts Hess to rest Sander because it's only going to keep you banging your head against a brick wall. You have to let it go."

Chapter Twenty Six

Returning to the inn Theo desperately wanted to make an urgent phone call. Before picking up the phone he thought about his last words with Sander. 'Your obsession has hit a dead end period. The child's jacket has left no trail and now it's really nothing more than a piece of ancient history.' He quickly regretted saying that, a sad look on Sander's face. The truth he knew was it was time to turn the jacket over to either the British or German authorities or donate it to a museum. There was only so much an amateur sleuth can accomplish he understood.

The call to High Meadows was a relief, the tension easing a bit hearing that Noah was progressing on his own schedule and doing well. Before he could ask the questions on his mind the line curiously went dead. He'd gotten up the nerve to ask if Noah had spoken but it was not to be.

Rather than calling back he went over some organizing in his mind. Spend two more days and no more with Sander, steering him if possible away from having to deal not with any Hess issues, If possible he might help Sander find living quarters where he might be safe. The long distance separation from Noah had become a heavier load to carry so no more than forty-eight hours he was convinced. Would finding a new place be difficult? Had it really been necessary to destroy Sander's ancestral home?

He needed a warm bath, to eat something light and sleep through the night but that would all have to wait. He was experiencing the pea in the mattress syndrome again, driven to calling the institute again. Saying hello the line was again disconnected. It didn't take a lot to push him closer to a nervous breakdown. Subsequent calls produced the same miserable results. On the final try he shouted in desperation before hang up that he had to speak with Dr. Ark.

Squeezing the phone so tightly his fingers cramped, a recurring headache returned with vengeance. Feeling like a hamster madly running around a wheel inside a cage, he was burning energy but going nowhere. The wheel slowed a bit when he heard Dr, Joan's voice, frustration still running rampant.

"I understand you called at three in the morning recently." The words caused Theo to blush. "Before I give you an update on Noah's progress I want to know if you're okay."

There was a bad case of shattered nerves he might confess, mostly due to the absence from Noah but also thoughts of leaving Sander alone. "I'm doing okay," he uttered, sensing Dr. Joan could hear grief three thousand miles away. He'd come to believe Dr. Joan always knew when he wasn't doing well, which was too often.

Assuring her several times he was alright he found it easier to talk about Sander and life in Eaglesham than himself. The more he rambled his voice sounded as if he were shouting through a megaphone. "How is Noah doing" he asked, slurring the words together unaware he'd just asked the question?

"First my friend take a few deep breaths and make yourself comfortable. I want you to settle down. After a few moments composing yourself I want you to clear your mind and listen without interruption. Noah is fine, period. He's well taken care of and getting lots of attention. I do have a curious question for you though. Did Noah ever have a pet dog?"

Of all the word things he'd expected to hear the subject of a dog was not one. It was so out of place it actually calmed him, nearly making him laugh. "Sorry, we've never owned a dog."

"We use therapy dogs at the institute and Noah's become quite fond of a certain Golden Retriever, spending much time with him. A dog has curative powers humans can't figure out so this is positive.

"Theo I sense Noah's days of being adrift are getting closer to the end. Picture a secure life preserver supporting him, keeping him afloat in a very stormy sea. He's a bright boy still adapting easily to the routines and doing what we expect. At our last team meeting everyone agreed the wall Noah erected was still quite formidable but things are changing. Take solace knowing we've worked with many children with similar trauma and in different ways they've all been helped. There's still a ticking time bomb inside but we're making progress defusing it."

Dr. Joan added there were few surprises and that Noah was making progress on his own time.

"Theo it's a breakthrough when a child enters this place without kicking and screaming. We can't read Noah's thoughts but as professionals we do have special insights. He's safely surrounded by wonderfully dedicated people making sure he's living in a stress free environment. That in itself will help him eventually deal with his loss.

"Day five presented some interesting changes all for the good. He began smiling a bit more and dressing early which told us he's ready to work and play. Treatment for trauma is a slow process, gentle nudges rather than a sudden shove. Childhood traumas create a heightened stress response to new situations, in this case the loss of mother and brother the catalyst. In a couple of days the team feels he'll be ready for deeper therapy but keep this in mind. It's not unusual for the silence to run a long course. If you were in his shoes you'd want to maintain that wall, protecting yourself as long as you could. Trauma does not go away on it's own so be patient and keep this in mind. Children are much more resilient than adults.

"The frightening event in Noah's young life cut deep. Working with children here we practice the three E's; the event causing the trauma, the experiential reaction to the trauma, and the after and often lingering effects of the trauma. Time is the best and safest treatment so there's no time limit. The team will meet again in four days so are you okay with what I've said?"

After a long pause Theo replied it was a lot to digest but he understood. "You know you can reach me at the inn in Eaglesham."

An air of sadness enveloped him when the call ended, muttering to himself why did this have to happen?

Chapter Twenty Seven

Returning to the town hall checking on Sander he spied the child sized flight jacket lying on the office desk. "The object of my obsession these days" said Sander with great tiredness in his voice. "You know Hess had a child but I doubt he was invited along on a perilous flight."

"What about a child of Adolf Hitler" Theo inquired? "There've been studies done to determine if his sperm was used to impregnate ideal Nordic women."

"I'm aware of those stories but it would be very hard to prove because so much time has passed. If you're curious Hess' son Wolfe, the offspring of Rudolf and Ilse was apparently their only child. There wasn't much written about him in his early years but he became known to the world recently because of his father's death. He's actually a hot issue today, mainly due to his rabid insistence his father had not committed suicide at Spandau Prison as reported, but was murdered by British intelligence. Wolfe said his father was finally silenced because of the fear he might reveal embarrassing accounts. I've ruled out Wolfe as a passenger but it's possible he might be the only one who knows the real truth and if he does, he's not letting on. He rarely talks to the press but when he does he staunchly defends his father.

"He would have been about five or six when his father flew away, this jacket far too large to be his. Did most of the Nazi leaders have children? Pure Germans were encouraged to have many children, a 1933 decree making it Illegal for women to have abortions. The names of the sons and daughters born to Nazi officials were kept secret so no harm would come to them after the war. During the last days of the war all records were destroyed. One of the lesser credible London newspapers claimed they had information a cleaning woman had an affair with a well known Lutwaffe pilot. If that were true there had to have been thousands of Lufwaffe pilots besides Hess. The article reported the unknown child like most others was eventually transported to one of the centers for unclaimed lebresborn children.

"Reporters in their new examination of Hess state unequivocally there are answers locked away in old Soviet files, not German or British. Why? Because the Soviets got to Berlin first during the final days of the war. One unproved assumption has Hitler fathering many children and if the dates are close to accurate, one son or daughter might have been twelve years old when Hess went airborne. I have a copy of a letter here written after he heard about the flight by son Wolfe.

'My father took off in his Messerschmitt 110 to Scotland to make a peace settlement.' The scribbling indicates the note was written in a very young child's handwriting, sent to a friend only two days after his father was captured. If the letter is legitimate it means Wolfe could not have been the passenger.

Chapter Twenty Eight

Both halfheartedly agreed pursuing Hess any further was a pipe dream, impossible to investigate Sander's theory about a passenger. Could there truly have been a passenger on Hess' flight?

"The jacket is quite unique Sander said contritely, "and if an expert analyzed the material I'm certain it would prove to be the real deal. Not to mention this happened fifty years ago" Sander added ruefully.

"Theo, Hess has been dead now for nearly two weeks and newspapers especially the ones with a reputation for stretching the truth are having a field day. They're conjuring up conspiracies and contriving sensational stories. Thank goodness Eaglesham has not been mentioned in any of the articles and that's much to my relief. These new stories unfortunately provide road maps for modern Neo-Nazi groups wishing to pay homage to Hess. Even though his body was secretly exhumed and cremated it still hasn't stopped neo-Nazi groups from gathering in places such as the cemetery.

"The name Floors Farm was mentioned in several articles published by one particular tabloid, the writer obviously misinformed because that was not the place where Hess fell to earth."

"Sander you and Eaglesham are quite fortunate the true site was mentioned in error otherwise the village might receive unwanted attention from extreme undesirables."

"I've read a lot over the years about Hess' travails after the helicopter whisked him away from my farm. I nearly have his entire itinerary memorized, getting picked up here to his end at Spandau. He was moved first to Busby East Renfrewshire where he refused to speak to anyone but the Duke of Hamilton. Next he was transported to the police station in Giffnock, about an hours drive from here. No record of any interrogation exists, possibly locked away forever. Days after that he was moved to the Maryhill Barracks in Glasgow, a military base remaining there just long enough to allow his injuries to heal. From there he was moved to Buchanan Castle where he allegedly spoke at length about Hitler's expansionary plans for the Soviet Union. He maintained he was an emissary from Hitler, declaring he had the authority to sign any treaty between Germany and England. If England agreed to his demands he emphasized, it would allow Germany free rein in Europe and in return, England could keep all her overseas territories.

"As to the other stops before the Tower of London became his home during the war years little is known, but he did spent time in several military hospitals for examinations."

A loud knock at the door caused both men to jump. Sander whispered say nothing and be absolutely still until whoever it is goes away.

"I know you're in there Sander McCann so open the damn door. I have something you might find very interesting."

"What is it" Sander growled?"

"I was here the other night when you spoke and it made me remember something I'd hidden away many years ago. I saved an old Glasgow newspaper article for what reason I can't recall but I thought about it when you spoke. You need to read this."

Allowed to enter Sander's private quarters, Tam McClean pulled an old yellowed Daily Record newspaper out of his bag, pointing to the publishing date of Tuesday May 13, 1941. The fragile paper spoke volumes about it's age. Theo and Sander moved closer to read the faded print.

In large bold print the headline declared Nazi Leader Flies to Scotland, **RUDOLF HESS IN GLASGOW.**

'Rudolf Hess, Hitler's right hand man fled Germany and is currently locked up in an unknown location in Glasgow. It was reported he was receiving treatment for a broken ankle and cuts and bruises. In a satchel he pulled out photographs to help establish his identity. An official statement issued from 10 Downing Street verified the story.

'Rudolf Hess, Deputy Fuhrer of Germany and party leader of the Nationalist Socialist Party crash landed his plane in Scotland under the following circumstances.' Sadly some of the wording was illegible due to the paper's age.

'The Nazi was discovered on the McCann farm in the village of Eaglesham, near Glasgow. Sander McCann, a ploughman by trade found Rudolf Hess. In his own words McCann related the details of his arrival exclusively for the Daily Record, the only newspaper on the scene.'

Sander turned bright red, hands trembling. "I never spoke to the press so this story is a complete falsehood." The story on page two insisted I suffered a nervous breakdown after the incident, another outright lie Sander shouted.

"I swear I never said those words nor did I speak with anyone other than British authorities. The story is completely made up. It's pure nonsensical and if I'd known about it at the time it went into print I would have raised hell. Nearly fifty years ago? I swear on my life I never spoke with any reporter. If Tam saved this old paper though there could be others who might have saved this poisonous piece and I'm certain it's on microfiche available to the public. I fear if this gets out we could easily become a destination for neo-Nazis." Oh Hell Sander lamented.

Chapter Twenty Nine

The feeding frenzy in the scandalous press for snippets of Hess' life was like blood in the water to sharks. Wolfe, Hess's son decided to talk to one particular newspaper two weeks after his father's death, no doubt because the paper offered more money than the others. He claimed the same government that tried to make his father a scapegoat resolutely sought to suppress the truth. 'The authorities were responsible for his murder, obviously to silence him but their conspiracy will not succeed. The murder of my father will not as they hope forever close the book on the Hess file. I am convinced in the future history and justice will absolve my father. His courage risking his life for peace, the long injustice he endured and his martyrdom will not be forgotten. He will be vindicated and his final words at the Nuremberg trial shall go down in history. I regret nothing. My father's murder was not only a crime against a frail and elderly man but a crime against historical truth. One day soon the truth will be known. I urge everyone to keep my father's fight for justice alive. The trial authorities declared in victory that my father was not formally charged at the Nuremberg trial with war crimes or crimes against humanity. Instead he was the one man who'd risked his life to secure peace, and incredibly he was found guilty of crimes against peace.'

When Tam left Theo asked Sander if anyone else knew about the child size jacket.

Forlornly Sander shook his head no.

"Are you certain none of the soldiers or British authorities were aware you received a gift?"

There was no response.

"Are you sure the jacket wasn't discovered during the searches of your home?"

"Trust me I told no one. There is one thing bothering me though. The poor soldier guarding my home might have searched while I slept. Could I have inadvertently mentioned the jacket when we talked? Absolutely not. You're the only living soul I've ever told. What about you when I sent it along to the States?"

"It remained in the box it was shipped in, taken out just once to compare the size to Noah's winter coat. Immediately after I re packed it under a heavy sweater and it stayed there until my flight back to Scotland. There was no way anyone in America knew what I possessed."

"Have you ever read Macbeth" Sander queried? If you did you'd recall the story's plot is a lot like this. It's a tragedy dramatizing the physical and psychological affects of political ambition by those seeking power for their own sake. Maybe that's all there is to say about Hess but I mean this with all sincerity. I have no other interest anymore in the man except to discover the truth about the jacket, even if it turns out to be nothing. There's urgency because if Tam had the newspaper stashed away in his home all these years others might have copies in their old scrapbooks. I fear notoriety because that libelous article might still be floating about out there.

"The jacket is a lighting rod to me Theo. Do you think I should turn it over to the British authorities and let them deal with it? Should we destroy it?"

"I hate you giving it up" Theo responded, "but that might be the best way to let go of this thing. I'm terribly sorry this problem literally fell into your lap. You and I however are dealing with more serious issues in our lives right now; you needing to find a place to live and me wanting a healthy

Noah. Sander I said it before but I truly think for your own sake it's time to put Hess aside, knowing that will not be easy. Maybe Hess' death will reveal more World War Two secrets and more answers will surface. The entire Hess saga will eventually die out one day and I suspect he'll just become a lost footnote in the story of Nazism. I need to go home soon so let's spend our time finding you a good place to live.

"Tell me about your plans for Noah, that sweet boy."

"Noah's in a residential treatment center. I agreed to a ten day period of therapy for Noah with one difficult condition. I had stay away during that time and the separation troubles me greatly. Remember, you're family too. Before returning home if you don't mind I'd love to see any documents in the town's records about our family. I promised Noah we'd fill in the family tree."

"This dam old newspaper makes me feel like I'm reading my obituary. I'll do whatever's possible to drop future dealings with the late Mr. Hess but no guarantee. I'll try like hell to evict him from my head and not allow him to run my life anymore. I'm going to miss you when you go Theo. You make sure you give that boy a big bear hug from me and Theo, all will be well one day. He's a nice boy and I trust one day he'll tell you he loves you very much,"

CHAPTER THIRTY

It was always unbearably frustrating calling the institute. Either Dr. Joan could not come to the phone or she was out for the day. Noah was doing well Dr. Joan's assistant reported, although Theo had no idea what doing well entailed. What happens if the silence becomes permanent he wondered? Would Noah keep his once beautiful life bottled up until irreparable damage could not be fixed? Was irreversible damage already done? The word doing well was positive but did little to ease the worry.

The last days with Sander were not productive, half heartedly searching into McCann family history. Theo dutifully took notes while Sander did his best deciphering old faded church records. At the end of their days together some progress was made, the branches and leaves of Noah's family tree filling. There should have been wonderment about the discoveries but the work failed to stir emotion. The only saving grace was the knowledge Noah's ten days would soon be over, hopefully discharged with a miracle cure.

Sander and Theo both sensed it was most likely the last time they'd be together. Sander was getting on in years, a victim like so many others caught up in the cruel Hess saga. As to what would become of the flight jacket it was agreed Sander would keep it, hoping there would be a right time to make a final decision.

On the flight home Theo mused if the plane crashed he would finally be at peace. The distraught look on his face drew the attention of one of the flight attendants, asking if he were alright. In a few hours he'd be home and on the phone with Dr. Joan, finding out if Noah spoke. It had to be all or nothing he believed, the absence of speech becoming heavier to bear every day.

Being home again was like entering a foreign setting, a house and not a place where a family once enjoyed the good life. Thoughts about selling the home nagged him, an empty house too large for just he and Noah, the good memories distant.

Deep breaths before calling the institute never helped, hoping for the best yet fearing the worst, the phone in his hand feeling like twisted barbed wire. Waiting for the receptionist he stared at the front door, recalling every painful minute when the police arrived with the dreadful news.

Dr. Joan said Noah had done well but that wasn't enough to ease the pins and needles he was feeling, not hearing the words Noah spoke was like a dagger to his heart. If Noah was talking those should have been her first words he sadly recounted. They were not and what followed left him uneasy. "Come in tomorrow morning at ten and we'll talk about Noah." Just like the see me message from the boss he thought.

Chapter Thirty One

Dr. Joan did not greet Theo but Dr. Becker.

"Before we discuss Noah I want you to understand a bit more about the work we do here. Parents often view therapy as a panacea and when the therapy doesn't work, it can be profoundly demoralizing."

Theo only heard the meaning, Noah had not been helped.

"We're not a hospital dealing with physical problems. I use the term mental illness not to alarm you but to help you understand we're dealing with a post-traumatic stress disorder, a mental issue. Often the first treatments don't always work but that's not the end. If we were dealing with heart disease we wouldn't throw our hands up and surrender if the first medication or procedure didn't yield positive results. With therapy it's the same thing. If one therapy fails there are other options."

The words were painful, suggesting Noah might not be able to be treated.

"I wish I could tell you how long it takes to obtain results for Noah but I can't. We've considered medication and Dr. Ark will fill you in about that. Every person is different and every mental health condition demands slightly different therapy. We're not practicing brain magic, we're teaching Noah how to manage his emotions. It might be time to combine medication with the therapy and we'll get to that shortly.

"I know it can be deeply frustrating when therapy doesn't work instantly but for Noah this is just the beginning and not an end. I want you to understand if Noah's symptoms continue much longer however the damage grows and it's highly unlikely it will not go away on it's own. Dr. Ark will take you through the steps we'd like to take next. The diagnosis is right on though; post traumatic stress disorder.

"Dr. Ark will also tell you Noah has worked successfully through the first of the three phases we've crafted specifically for him. The first was feeling safe with stabilization and we achieved that. If you decide to continue treatment which I recommend the next phase is getting Noah to process the trauma and learn how to reconnect with the world around him."

Not hearing what he wanted to hear Dr. Becker did not need to say Noah had not said a word. The down look on Theo's face paused the discussion so Dr. Becker could move his chair closer. There was a warm softness in his words.

"We always address a child with compassion. Trauma work can be precarious and unpredictable but we're prepared. Don't give up the ship because we've certainly not. When I mentioned safety and stability earlier, Dr. Ark and staff have not tried to get Noah to relive his traumatic memory, agreeing Noah was not ready at this time. Trauma in all people whether young or old brings up feelings of shame and sometimes self-harm. We've made Noah feel safe and that in itself is success. Dr. Ark is waiting for you in her office and she'll fill you in on the distance Noah has traveled and where we go from here. I know this is not what you hoped to hear but after you talk with Dr. Ark and reconnect with Noah, I think you'll be at ease."

CHAPTER THIRTY TWO

"Dr. Becker is an extraordinary human being and I would not be working here if not for him. Theo here's the situation. First, Noah's a wonderfully curious child and I've grown quite attached to him. You probably heard Dr. Becker say Noah's ten days here have for the most part been beneficial and productive. There's no way to measure how much of the protective shell we've broken down but we believe it's been weakened. All the members of Noah's team agree with that aspect. I've said this often but time is the only restraint. He's young and resilient and his demeanor tells us he feels safe and cared for. Once a child feels that way it's easier to transition to the next phase of treatment. If you're curious how he spent his play time he must have drawn several hundred butterflies, each colored beautifully, each with the words for dad or Sander and surprisingly some for me. His reading comprehension level is far beyond what one might expect from an eleven year old. Your son took it upon himself to read every children's book in our library.

"It's my hope that you'll allow us to continue working with Noah. I know of no other institute in the nation measuring up to our work with cases like this. I think you'll see a different boy when you reunite and appreciate the hard work he's done. The pain he feels is deep but instead of suffocating, I think he's working hard to breath. He's certainly not ready to give up and neither are we. Spend as much time as you'd like with him after I take you to his room. Are we okay so far?"

"I guess" was obviously the answer Dr. Joan not want to hear. "I often forget to be grateful Dr. Joan. You came into our lives in such a strange and fateful way so I guess my first question is do you want Noah staying here beyond the ten days? If you do can I somehow get involved or visit? It'll break my heart to leave him here again but I'll do it if it helps the healing process."

"I was saving the best for last. Noah will no longer be treated in-patient but have no fear, he's going home with invisible crutches to help him when he stumbles. You're not going home alone. You're taking your son home so the two of you can get on with your lives. Does that mean the connection to High Meadows is over? Not in the least because if you'll agree, Noah will become out-patient which entails being dropped off in the morning and picked up at night. Weekends are yours. We can start after the weekend on Monday if you'll agree. He'll only need a day pack with a change of clothes. We'll ask you to come in for a consult once a week so you can meet with the entire team. Phase two begins Monday meaning it's time to introduce the traumatic event very gently. Processing the trauma has to be done slowly because we don't want to make the situation worse. Call me at this number where I can be reached twenty-four hours a day if you have questions or concerns. This is not the end but the beginning of intense work. By the way you'll be taking home a carton but don't open it until you're safely home.

Chapter Thirty Three

Noah said not one word during the ride but Theo felt less upset, sensing Noah was more at peace. The boy gobbled down a hot dog when they stopped as if he hadn't eaten in days. That was a change Theo noted because normally he'd just push his food around the plate. The boy seemed more animated either because he'd been touched by Dr. Ark and her team or he'd missed his dad.

For the first time in weeks walking into the house felt a tad like home again, although still a distant feeling. It somehow seemed warmer and a bit brighter after the many long and dark days. Theo wanted to talk about the accident but abandoned the thought, cautioned by Doctor Becker he wasn't ready.

Noah explored his room, looking for familiar things, a grin on his face seeing something important. When the phone rang Theo jumped because it rarely happened these days. Guessing it was Dr. Joan asking about the homecoming he was wrong. A loud buzzing noise on the line made it difficult to hear. When it finally stopped he clearly heard the words this is Mrs. Tavish, Mr. McCann's assistant at the town hall in Eaglesham. "Is this Mr. Theo McCann?"

This can't be good was his only thought, a cautious yes the answer. Curiosity was replaced with a gripping apprehension.

"Mr. McCann your uncle wanted me to check and see if you got home safely. There's also another reason for my call. He asked me to give you the name of his lawyer because he's changed his will. Have no fear because he's well, just wanting you to know there's something in it for you to help take care of your son."

The words were puzzling but thankful it wasn't a call with a new problem. Expressing thanks to Mrs. Tavish he asked to have Sander get in touch with him if he needed anything.

Hanging up and peeking into Noah's room there was something to be thankful for. The boy looked happy to be home, the bound carton a reminder of something special to be opened.

Gathering Noah up in his arms he said how much he loved and missed him. The response was different this time. Noah hugged back.

Opening the carton was like Christmas morning at home with family, curious what might be inside. There was a look of knowing on Noah's face, pure Christmas Theo supposed. Opening the carton and reaching inside he gathered an armful of paper, all the art work done by Noah at the institute. "You were a very busy boy" he said, greeted by a wonderful smile and nod. "Lets see what we have here."

Theo commented on each drawing, Noah seemingly delighted with himself. The work was quite good Theo realized.

"Is this a drawing of Sander" he asked? Noah nodded, another sign of progress. "It's a great still life. Do you know what that means?" Noah shrugged his shoulders.

Another drawing had Sander sitting by the fire place, a stack of peat on the hearth and a glowing fire. The next five drawings found Sander in the center, a young boy by his side, his dad smiling from across the room. Each drawing brought Theo back to the room where he and Sander shared the remarkable story of Hess. Other's were filled with outdoor scenes, a boy running after butterflies and a woman chasing after him.

Theo was overcome, each new picture a portrait of their time spent in Eaglesham. Dr. Joan chasing after young Noah and expressions of wonder on their faces took his breath away. Reaching for the last of the drawings in the carton Theo saw a noticeable change in tone and composition. A picture of Sander painted a sad look on his face, the background blackened. The next drawings were also mostly done in black, faces showing what seemed to be sorrow and fright.

The great affection for Sander was obvious as were the bright colors of Dr. Joan running, long auburn hair flying behind her. There was great contrast from the bold colors to the heavy blackness. The pictures of trees with green leaves with smiling faces touched him deeply. The blackened drawings told another story. Realizing Noah had fallen asleep he tiptoed from the room walking straight to the telephone, wanting to tell Dr. Joan about the drawings. Fortunately she was still at work charting. "You opened the carton I bet" were her first words.

"Yes" he said, at a loss for the right words describing how they made him feel. "It was very obvious Noah took in all the goings on in Eaglesham, communicating beautifully through the artwork. Some of the drawings raised a few questions so I wanted to call and ask if you had a little time to chat."

"Of course. From the drawings you see Noah was hard at work, art the process used to unlock things he cannot yet express. This is a classic method allowing Noah to tell us what's going on in the inner mind of the young boy. Tell me what's on your mind?"

"Well the drawings clearly show his great affection for Sander and the joys of running outdoors looking for butterflies with you. Is this a prelude to talking anytime in the near future?"

"You know I don't put time limits on treatment. What else is going on.

"In a couple of weeks I'm going to ask permission to take time from Noah's therapy and hopefully return to Eaglesham with him. The work you've done and the emotions Noah now expresses through art makes me believe he's actually on the road to recovery. Do you think a pause in treatment is worth perusing or should I forget it? I'd like to meet up with you and the team to get your thoughts about this, meaning is he healthy enough to leave treatment for some extended days.

"Don't get your hopes up about traveling just yet. Noah is a very strong boy and from what we've seen at the institute he'll be okay. There's much to be done but if past successes are any indication, Noah does have what it takes to break his wall down. We'll talk about taking time out when I believe Noah is ready."

PART THREE

CHAPTER THIRTY FOUR

Life as usual was on hold. Every morning he and Noah drove to High Meadows and every afternoon rode home together. There were subtle but noticeable changes in Noah's demeanor, but at times the silence became exceptionally frustrating, no two steps forward and one step back he acknowledged. It was as if Noah was stuck in neutral and unable to get into first gear. Small changes were obvious to Noah's team but to an outside observer, he was just a shy happy kid with not much to say.

The first week went well Dr. Joan announced, "Progress was measured by the nodding or shaking of his head and the reactions to yes and no. There were more observable body gestures expressing approval or disapproval."

Theo thought little about Hess during the outpatient days, however he appeared as a fixture during the night visiting in dreams. Sander always insisted the man had a way of taking up space in one's head and Theo became a true believer. A full month after Hess's death the buzz merciful finally began to run it's course, with the exception of the outrageous supermarket tabloids extolling such notions that Hess was alive and leading a good life in a village somewhere in South America.

A return to Scotland with Noah weighed heavily on his mind, picturing a grand reunion after one long lonely drive home after dropping Noah at the institute. They both missed Sander, Noah's attachment obvious in the volume of pictures devoted to the man. Theo couldn't fully explain it but the two seemed to have touched each other's souls, understanding each other in a special way. Many of Noah's outpatient days were spent with the art teacher who took great pleasure watching Noah move tiny brushes about a blank canvass, creating what she called emotional art.

Each night Noah brought most of his art work home, other pieces given to his team as gifts. The team relished those snippets into the mind of a boy silenced by the great trauma in his life. Butterflies continued to be a main theme, taking second fiddle to the self portraits and drawings of a wise and sympathetic older man with white hair.

During week two of outpatient therapy the team began to touch on the incident preceding the muteness, asking Noah simple yes or no questions. The staff didn't tiptoe around the fateful day but when they saw an opening they took advantage. Photographs taken of Noah at the institute showing different reactions or expressions were shown to him. A photo of a troubling look on his face or a photo with a look of relief or respite got different reactions.

Dr. Joan ran a small group therapy half hour with certain children including Noah, using doll's faces manipulated to show happiness, sadness, cheerfulness, and thoughtfulness. One of the more difficult days in week two involved a guest speaker, a young child who'd not spoken in nearly a year after seeing his father commit suicide. The boy now able to speak talked about what it felt like to be troubled and saddened, wanting to scream and cry but unable to utter a sound.

When Noah came home that particular night he went straight to his room, pulling the covers over his head refusing to come to the dinner table for his favorite meal. Theo lay down next to him all night until it was time to get up and start a new day.

The daily rides to High Meadows became routine, Hess a mere afterthought. At the end of the week Noah decided he would ask the team if it would be possible to reunite the boy and his great uncle, someone very dear and important to Noah.

The meeting was held on a Friday after working hours, headed by Dr. Becker who asked the team the risks and rewards of halting therapy for five or six days. The consensus was mixed, each team member explaining reasons for either waiting longer or considering the journey a different kind of therapy benefiting Noah.

Dr. Becker asked Dr. Joan to conclude the discussion, declaring she would have the final say on the matter.

"We're at a critical juncture with Noah and I've listened to all the risks and rewards the team has expressed. I have a special and unique relationship with Noah and I've taken that into consideration. My decision is yes because the boy's great uncle Sander might just be the key allowing Noah to speak. Theo let us know your plans as to when and how long. I thank each of you for your input allowing me to give dad and son my okay and blessing.

Expecting a negative response Theo became so overwhelmed he broke down sobbing. Fighting to hold back tears he suddenly stopped and began laughing like a madman. The laughter grew contagious and soon the entire team joined in and cheered. "God speed" said Dr. Becker, "We are adjourned."

CHAPTER THIRTY FIVE

Theo gave himself until Sunday to make it official because he wanted to observe Noah carefully to see if he was ready for a long journey, air tickets for he and Noah on standby. Closing up the house was easy, stopping the mail and packing the only extras. The last piece was how and when to get in touch with Sander which had become increasingly more difficult. The plan was to fly out a week from Saturday night into Glasgow, arriving Sunday in Eaglesham, expecting the town most likely closed up tight. He tried calling Sander with the news but all he could do was leave messages to call him. There was still time he understood, because he wanted Noah to experience another week at High Meadows.

He thought about calling Franz reserving a room which was probably not necessary, but more importantly to ask on the sly how his uncle was doing. Calling there was no answer at the inn, something feeling odd.

He called Dr. Joan to tell her that Noah would be coming in Monday, the trip not scheduled until the following Saturday.

"Are you calling because you've changed your mind?"

Theo laughed, an emotion missing in his life. "Could you possibly stop by on you're way home one day next week because I need some advice. Nothing pressing so any evening during the week if you could make it. I'll even prepare Noah's favorite meal a way for us to thank you for all you've done.

To his surprised she said when she finished her work she'd come by that evening. Feeling like a teenager who'd just asked for a first date, he caught the obvious smirk on Noah's face. Nothing wrong with your ears he said.

Feeling somewhat upbeat even though Noah's progress was painfully slow, life as always was iffy. "Here's the plan for next week Noah because I have a special treat." The look on Noah's face told him let the cat out of the bag.

"I've decided we're going to make another long field trip to you know where. Eaglesham in Scotland. This time we'll hopefully discover more about our family history and what's more, you'll get to see your great Uncle Sander again."

There was a visible reaction when he'd explained the journey Noah's face lighting up. A long warm hug cemented the deal. "And I will let you stay up late tonight because someone very special will dropping by in a few hours. For the briefest of moments Theo thought the boy would respond.

"I'd like to bring a special gift for Sander so do you think you might put something together for him? You've got all those wonderful drawings in your room so why not make an album just for Uncle Sander." The suggestion was met with life in Noah's eyes.

Just after eight Dr. Joan arrived, Noah running to the door attaching himself in a heartfelt hug, "I missed you" she said. "Did your father tell you about another field trip that you're going to take in a week?"

Theo felt emotions getting the best of him, glad he'd told Noah about Scotland. Noah took Dr. Joan's hands pulling her excitedly toward his bedroom, the bed covered with drawings of Sander and the makeshift cardboard album cover he'd crafted.

"You keep working on the album and I'll just be spending a little time with your dad."

Theo had experienced many roller coaster rides the past months but suddenly life felt more like a gentle merry go round. Life had fewer sharp edges and seemed a bit more manageable, something he never thought possible. "Dr. Joan thank you for all you've done to help us. I can't imagine what life would be like if it weren't for you."

"Theo I was going to wait until your return from Scotland to let you in on something but your call made it the right time. The institute will be going through some significant changes in the next weeks and months but there's nothing to be alarmed about. This might be the best time to fill you in. Dr. Becker, my mentor and teacher and friend is leaving High Meadows in two months. He was offered an opportunity to run a department at the NIA, the prestigious National Institute of Health. He offered me the opportunity to take his place as director of the institute cautioning me not to answer until I'd done a great deal of soul searching. In truth I could have given him an answer at that moment but he wouldn't have it. I knew those words would be uttered one day but I could never envision High Meadows without him. I said yes I would think about it over the weekend and we'd talk Monday.

"Because of my fondness for Noah I'm going to tell you what I've decided. In the past Dr. Becker had many generous job officers to manage world class institutions both here and abroad. He turned them all down for a variety of reasons I won't go into. So this is the predicament for me. I don't want to be the director because I'm not a paper pusher. I enjoy my work and I can't see myself tied to a desk. As of right now I'm planning to stay on at least until Dr. Becker's departure, then hopefully going into private practice. Perhaps down the road I might even join a university to do research."

The lightening bolt out of the blue hit with unexpected force. There was no mother in Noah's life, no woman providing nurturing at a critical time in Noah's life. Dr. Joan was a God send. Theo felt shaken, wondering if it was the end of her work with Noah.

"First of all I'm not going anywhere right now. I have a full case load at High Meadows and much unfinished business. I won't take on any new cases starting Monday though and after I've done all I can with the last child it'll be the right time to walk away. I plan on using the next few months setting up an office where I will do private therapy and some group sessions. By the look on your face I see you're obviously troubled by this, it certainly has to be upsetting."

"This will sound terribly selfish Dr. Joan but I fear without you Noah will regress and never be whole again. I told you once we'd seen many therapists, most suggesting let nature run it's course. The moment you so unexpectedly came into Noah's life changed everything. From the get go on the plane you've had a profound impact on me and Noah and I was so inexpertly fortunate to meet you. You gave me hope when there was really none, saying it was possible to crack the outer defensive shell and that Noah would speak again. What should I tell Noah?"

"You don't need to tell him anything right now. He's got Scotland to look forward to and he's still outpatient at High Meadows at least for another two months. Nothing will change so we continue our work and when it's time to leave I hope we'll have torn Noah's wall down. If you'd like I can continue working with Noah in private sessions, assured I won't bill you as a reward for being my first patient. There's one more thing on my mind I need to explain, something has affected my good judgment at work.

"I've broken one of the cardinal rules of therapy which is to be subjective all times and not make the work personal. Once that happened I lost my objectivity and my judgments became clouded. I'm not doing what's best for my patients right now, with few exceptions. I'm not sure why I became so attached to your son but I can say honestly it hasn't affected Noah's counseling. It has however affected my work with other children which is unfair and wrong. I've discussed this with Dr. Becker who said he knew for some time but wanted me to figure this out on my own. He praised my work, especially my credo no child ever left behind. I care very much for your Noah and after I've cut ties with the institute, I'd like to continue working with him. Have I confused you enough?"

The headache that struck like a rampaging locomotive told him he was.

"I didn't realize that you were treating Noah different because all I cared about was him getting better. I sensed you two had a good and meaningful relationship so I'm sorry for your predicament. I began praying again at night, thanking God for Dr. Joan Ark. Did I ever tell you that one night I dreamed about the real Noah's Ark, looking very much like Sander reaching down to fetch a drowning boy from the water. I'd forgotten about that until just now."

Theo's emotions were riding on his skin. Patting his beating heart he hoped the gesture would suffice because he could not form the right words. When neither could think what to say next Noah came out of his room, album in hands.

"I'm certain you'll both have a wonderful time away so when you pick up Noah next Friday before you leave stop by my office. I have something I'd like you to bring Sander from me. I'll say goodnight to Noah and tell him that this is going to be a very special week.

Chapter Thirty Six

Arriving in Glasgow and soon on their way to Eaglesham in a rental car, Theo felt more at home there than in his own house. The familiar villages along the route were comforting sights, sadly a reminder Sander had no real home anymore, the thought somewhat dampening the homecoming. Driving over the old stone bridge and seeing the sign welcome to Eaglesham was a warm sight.

At the airport Theo tried calling the inn to let know Franz he was returning with Noah and could he reserve the very same room they'd shared on their first visit. There was no immediate response from Franz, only muffled talk probably with Greta he thought checking on the availability. Waiting for a response Theo had the odd feeling Franz was hedging. Was the inn overbooked? What seemed an interminable amount of time passed until Franz said he'd have the room ready, then hung up abruptly. Theo thought they'd been disconnected but he recognized an obvious hang up. It was nothing he thought, just caught Franz at a difficult or busy time.

Just as their first arrival on a Sunday a month earlier the town square was empty. Walking into the inn with their small bags they waited nearly a half hour for Franz to finally take his position at the reception desk. There was no jocularity, strictly business including the question will that be cash or credit. Greta was no where to be seen. Maybe there was trouble in their lives but it was none of his business he understood, slowly making their way to the room. Something wasn't quite right at the inn he believed. With no guests it probably had to do with money, He hadn't expected to be feted like a returning conquering hero but there was no usual light banter or the usual good camaraderie. No welcoming drink from Greta? No armload of old peat to warm the room? No invitation to the special Sunday banquet laid out for the townsfolk? There were more important things to stew over he knew and it wouldn't let it dampen the good feelings of being back.

There was no traditional feast, no salad sandwiches from Greta and no peat. With the village tightly closed up Theo felt fortunate they'd swiped extra snacks from the steward's cart during the flight. The room was cold making it necessary to huddle under extra blankets. Theo couldn't wait for the town hall to open in another day when hopefully Franz would be more civil.

In the morning there were more cold reactions from Franz. Still no Greta and worse, no breakfast. At ten sharp he and Noah walked up the town hall stairs, stomachs growling making them laugh, grateful the front door was unlocked. Noah ran ahead to the closed door behind the empty reception desk knocking loudly. Obviously Franz had not gotten the word to Sander because there was no Sander. Noah looked puzzled, a new look. He was certainly not the shell he was on their first visit. More loud knocking finally got results.

Through the closed door came irritated words. "No business today. Can't you read the sign? Come back tomorrow."

Theo was aghast. Unexpectedly great sounds of laughter burst forth from Noah to his delight. It was Theo's turn to knock with the words we're not here on business. We're here because we're family.

Before the last word was out the door opened. Noah leaped into Sander's arms, hanging on with all his might. Sander was totally overwhelmed, the realization Theo and Noah were actually there taking time to settle in.

"Noah my boy I have missed you terribly. Why didn't your father tell me you were coming to visit again?"

If there was a time and place for Noah to speak after months of silence it was that moment. Theo prayed but it was not to be.

Theo often pictured Sander as Santa, not because of his flowing white beard but because of his chortling. "Come sit down by the fire" Sander offered. "Tell me what brought you two to Eaglesham again."

"To be honest," Theo answered, "it was because Noah in his own special way told me he missed you terribly. He hasn't spoken yet but we are making good progress. He let me know through drawings he'd made at school he wanted to be with you again so here we are. Noah show Sander your album."

There were tears all around as Sander carefully turned each page. Noah took up his old work assignment, tossing more peat into the dying fire brightening the room. Not a word was spoken while Sander studied each picture. When he came to the last he closed the album telling Noah it was the finest art work he'd ever seen. "You have made an old man quite happy. I thank the Lord you came into my life."

Noah peeked around the room, Theo and Sander knowing what he was looking for. The butterfly net was still there, the expression on Noah's face speaking volumes.

"When Noah came home after his ten day stay at his special school he immediately looked for his comforting belongings. Your old butterfly net is like a third arm to the boy."

"You're very lucky to have Noah and he's lucky to have you Theo." The words made him choke up once again.

After the usual hot chocolate Noah went out with the butterfly net, still searching for the largest butterfly in all of Scotland. "Don't stray too far young man because this isn't my property and don't stay out too long." Noah smiled, another small step forward.

"I'm sorry my home is gone because it would have been nice having you stay with me. How long are you fixing to be here?"

179

"We're here for another five or six days Sander. I have much to tell you about Noah's therapy and the new expectations. Remember Dr. Joan?" Sander nodded, his trusty pipe being worked on.

"Noah is now out-patient at the school and Dr. Joan continues to work with him on the healing process. It's a long tough road but I do believe we're making progress. I'll fill you in later but first how are you feeling and what have you been up to? I loath to bring up our nemesis but I'd like to know if he's still renting space as an unwanted guest in your head."

"As a matter of fact I've been doing a fair amount of work, still trying to pull pieces together, mostly about the jacket. I freely admit I'm fixated on the jacket which reminds me, did you bring it along?"

"Of course. I'll get it out of my backpack."

"That's the last and most perplexing issue for me now, the rest I'm through with. I've pretty much given up fishing for answers to cloudy parts of his life, saving that for the so called experts. If Hess had never given me the damn jacket I swear he'd have been out of my life decades ago. I've always believed Hess had good reason to pass it along to me, believing it was more than an act of appreciation. Maybe he just wanted it kept safe for reasons I couldn't guess. The jacket's a cancer Theo, growing continually in my mind, not allowing me to be at peace. Since we last talked inside the old homestead I've tried to stay busy with town business, something I'd been slacking off. It's part intuition and curiosity but I find myself continually ruminating and dissecting Hess' life, particularly the time spent with me. I have absolutely no proof but I have this overpowering feeling that after spending nearly a half century with the man living in my head, there could have been a passenger on the plane. Sadly there's not a shred of evidence.

"There are a few certainties Theo. The jacket was certainly tailored for a child, possibly the same age as your Noah. If there was a passenger I think often about what might have happened to him? Did he, assuming it was a young boy because of the jacket, simply vanish? Could the passenger also have parachuted? My recollection of the day is that the winds were strong and possibly carrying him far away out of my line of sight. The passenger if there was one could not have weighed more than sixty or seventy pounds, unlike Hess's so its conceivable someone much lighter could have fallen far from the plane's crash site. He was not aboard when the plane crashed, something I knew for certain with my own eyes.

"Here's a crazy theory. The passenger if he existed, was probably dazed like Hess, most likely in shock on very unfamiliar ground. He could have run in panic, most likely unhurt, hoping to find Hess but ending up getting hopelessly lost. Why would Hess bring a child along on such a perilous journey? You know he was an ace pilot and he was very sure of himself so I'm certain he foresaw no danger.

"If I presuppose there indeed was a passenger drifting far from the crash site, it raises the question why didn't someone see the parachute and rush to help him? Hess never hinted someone accompanied him, nor has anyone else raised that possibility. If you were a pilot bringing a ten or twelve year old on a dangerously long flight, wouldn't you want to know if your passenger survived?

"Suppose Hess believed the child perished in the crash? That issue was settled when we searched the wreckage seeing no body. So why did he insist I go to the wreckage site with him? Only the tail section was whole, the rest a tangle of metal. I still recall the wild look in his eyes telling me he feared what he might or might not find. I was ordered, not asked to search the woods near my home but he never told me what to look for. If the definitive truth ever comes out about the true nature of Hess' exploit, it'll answer one of the war's greatest mysteries. Someone knows the entire truth and has all the answers but like Hess, he or she will always live in the shadows.

"Theo, ever heard of something called Project Thor? Maybe not because very few people were privy to it and most of the paperwork connected to the project was destroyed during the last days of the Nazi regime.

"Hess and his wife had a child named Wolfe as you know but he would have been too young to travel, possibly three or four years old at the time Hess made the flight. But Project Thor? It was actually a Nazi artificial insemination program set up in a specially built hospital building deep in the Bavarian Mountains, part of the Alps. It was a top secret lab where newborns were monitored, the result of egg fertilization with a donor in order to create the perfect Aryan race. Sperm donors were chosen carefully, their names later erased for obvious reasons. There were rumors then and now that Hitler might have fathered one or several of those children.

"The information I gleaned claimed hundreds of women between the ages of eighteen and twenty-seven were racially selected. After their baby was born he or she was transferred to the research complex in the Alps. At the time of Hess' flight there would have been as many as twenty children conceived, all about Noah's age. One of them might have accompanied Hess. Why did he want or need a passenger? I have a few thoughts about that too.

"Why is there no documentation for Project Thor? The answer is it was all destroyed in May of 1945, just weeks before the German surrender. Himmler ordered the building destroyed and the remaining children given to peasant families in Bavarian and Austrian villages. Was it possible one or many or even all the children around Noah's age were the result of Hitler's sperm? Sounds fantastic but the project was an integral part of the glorious Nazi-German scheme for a new world. Hitler's child on that plane?" If I suggested that to anyone I'd be deemed daft."

"One of the reason's for Hess's flight might have been to ensure a true heir to the Third Reich remained in a safe place surviving the war. If all went according to plans, the child could eventually becoming the savior of a new Germany after Hitler. Much remains secret in the British Archives and as long as they remain secreted, the world will never know the precise nature of Hess' mission. Two days before Hess' flight he had a private four hour meeting with Hitler and you can speculate about that for a long time.

"Hess' death was ruled suicide but even that's debatable. He was interned in the family grave and later exhumed. Since my name and farm were falsely identified in one of the British newspapers I now fear where Hess first touched down is public knowledge.

"During his forty years in the Spandau Prison Hess was not allowed to talk openly to anyone about his mission, a permanent gag order issued and the reason? Even today his mission could still turn into a great embarrassment for the British government, possibly leading to the royal family. I'll just say this and we'll move on. As long as material relating to Hess' mission remains secret the world will not know the precise nature of his peace proposal."

"Sander how certain are you there truly could have been a passenger? There's no hard evidence, a second parachute was never sighted and no one in the village or surrounding towns acknowledged seeing a young boy wandering aimlessly."

"I'm only building a case Theo. I didn't make this all up. Think about the child's jacket. If you were Hess on a secretive mission why bring along a child's jacket? Why not an autographed photo of Herr Hitler?"

"If what you say has merit why wasn't the boy been discovered?"

"Because he was probably taken in, prearranged by someone in the area, possibly plotted by British authorities favorable to the Nazi cause. Some theorists believe the British government was in on the plot all the time. What leads credence to this is the fact the RAF fighter planes were certainly capable of shooting down a German warplane but they didn't. The British should have been on high alert yet Hess soared untouched across the British Isles as if he were on a Sunday flight. Some very credible authorities believe Hess's plane went undetected because the British had arranged the entire plot. The Duke was questioned by none other than Churchill himself so what could they have discussed? Was Hess more intent on getting to the Duke's estate not to deliver a peace proposal, but possibly to shepherd a young boy into the hands of a Nazi sympathizer.? That could explain why the child was never seen by anyone wandering the countryside."

"I don't know Sander but the more you talk this up, the more I'm firmly fixated on the fact that without a shred of evidence your story would merely make a great piece of fiction. Since the British government isn't going to release secreted documents anytime soon and Churchill and the Duke are long dead, all you've got is the making of a good spy novel, which happens to be my field."

Sander snorted, shaking his head, a wry look.

"Oh yes one more thing that ought to be tossed into this simmering pot. In the late 1930's and early 40's there were rumors that many Brits, particularly nobility and aristocratic were secretly and not so secretly Nazi sympathizers. There's very strong evidence the extended royal family believed in Hitler for good reasons, such as he'd destroy Bolshevism. There's been much written over the years about who in the royal family were closeted Nazis. I'm not casting dispersions at the Duke but it's a fact he and Hess spent time commiserating at the 1936 Berlin Olympics, remaining life long acquaintances. You can understand why I don't sleep well."

Theo realized he'd forgotten about Noah, sending a course of panic through his body. He'd been gone for nearly an hour, possibly lost or worse hurt he fretted. "I'll be right back Sander. I'm going to run out and look for Noah."

Before getting to the door Noah walked in, a knowing smile, eyes aglow. Where's the butterfly net Theo asked? Noah shrugged his shoulders. Did you find the biggest butterfly in all of Scotland and lose the net Sander queried?

The expressive smile grew even bigger, Noah dashing back outdoors.

"I guess the boy found a good one" Sander said. "He looks awfully excited." Both men were convinced a special butterfly had indeed been captured and were about to see it. Noah's giggling was nothing short of a miracle to Theo, sad Noah's butterfly assistant Dr. Joan wasn't there to see the catch.

The door to the office slowly opened, Noah seemingly taking much delight in prolonging the anticipation.

Noah maneuvered the empty net end through the door and to Sander and Theo's stunned looks, on the other end was Dr, Joan. Noah couldn't control his laughter, a truly heartfelt sound. In awe Theo stood up so quickly he banged his head on one of the low wooden beams. Rubbing his head he joked the pain told him he wasn't dreaming.

"You're a sight to behold" Theo finally managed to say, "Why aren't you at work?"

"I am" was the reply. "A little birdie said Noah needed me so I came. Theo, the moment Noah entered High Meadows he understood no matter day or night, no matter what I was doing I'd always be there for him. When I came to your home to tell you about the changes at High Meadows I didn't realized you'd be leaving for Scotland in a week. Do you recall Noah spending a good deal of his time in his room when I visited? He was busy writing me a note accompanying a new picture. Without my knowing he tucked it into the pocket of my overcoat. I didn't discover it until I got home. See for yourself."

Both men stared at the picture and the accompanying words. Two men, a woman and a small boy were holding hands in a circle, gazing out the window at a large body of blue water. Far offshore a slender neck appeared, it's head high into the sky.

"That must be Nessie in Loch Ness," Sander said laughing. "Is that right Noah?" The question was answered with a nod.

"Noah drew many pictures for Sander Dr. Joan said, someone he's become quite fond of. A good number of pictures drawn were Nessie doing what sea monsters do I assume. The note said we should look for him."

"During a session I asked him if he'd like to go back to Scotland someday to travel to the lake searching for Nessie. That day I promised if he ever returned to Scotland I'd be there with him sharing that great adventure, so here I am. I hadn't planned on this trip but Noah has a way of tugging at my heart. Remember what we talked about when we chatted at your house that evening? I didn't realize you were leaving in a week so on my way home I vowed to keep my word. If Noah said he needed me, I'd be there.

"I can only stay for the weekend because I have a much casework to do and I'm behind on my work. Being here however is important for Noah's well being. Needless to say I'll need your permission to take Noah up to the loch maybe this afternoon, returning late Sunday afternoon. I've got an evening flight back to the States that night I can't miss. With some luck we'll spot Nessie but more importantly, it'll give me an opportunity to work with Noah and give you a chance to spend time alone with your uncle. What say you?"

Noah dashed over to his father, a pleading and rather persuasive look in his dark eyes. Theo wished the moment could last forever, his turn to pause as if he were thinking it over. With a wink and smile he nodded, saying yes.

"Noah take Dr. Joan back to the inn and pack an overnight bag. Don't forget the toothpaste and if you look in the top drawer of the dresser you'll find my camera. Take good care of it. I'm very excited for you and sincerely hope Nessie pokes her head out of the water so you can see her. You be a good boy and I'll see you Sunday afternoon. Dr. Joan, I don't know how to thank you for this kind offer and for everything you've done. No argument on this. I'll pay for the car rental and the plane fare. I don't know where we'd be if we didn't have you so this might sound corny but you truly are a saint.

CHAPTER THIRTY SEVEN

When Dr. Joan and Noah drove away Theo felt at peace, an overworked mind at dead calm.

"Sander join me for dinner later at the inn on me with one condition. Neither of us mentions the world of Rudolf Hess from the time we sit down until we get up again."

"Agreed, at least I'll try."

"I'd rather talk about our family in the time I have left here. I'd also like to tell you about my wife and other son Gabe. I rarely talk about them because it's still terribly painful but I really want you to get to know them. Can you handle a conversation without a third person sitting at out table?"

Sander laughed saying three's a crowd anyway and Hess was not invited to dinner.

"I'm going to go back to the inn and put my hiking boots and backpack on. I'd like to do some exploring on my own, searching for a place to sit and rest and even cry some of my sadness away. See you at seven okay?"

A few steps onto one of the town's well kept trails felt magical, noting a smart bounce in his step right away. For the better part of many months life had been on hold, constantly fighting to keep his head above water and the strength to chase bad thoughts away. Talking to Sander about his family would make things better he hoped.

Discovering a clearing with a floor of deep thick peat moss near a slow moving stream he decided it was the idea place to cool tired feet. He laughed aloud, the water reminding him of Nessie's home. Whatever it takes even if it's a mythical monster he said aloud. Time stood still surrounded by nature, the perfect spa and rehab he was convinced. Wiping tears away he stared at the heavens vowing to his wife that he would always take care of Noah. He missed his wife terribly, especially just before falling asleep each night. When the sun began setting the light coming through the great oaks and pines turned golden. Making his way back to the inn he felt rested, hoping Fritz and Greta would prepare something very special for them.

Franz was obviously still in a snit acting icy and aloof. Instead of friendly banter it was strictly business. "Greta is in the kitchen" he snapped "and she doesn't like anyone around when she's cooking." That was the extent of their conversation.

It felt as if a bucket of cold water had been dumped on him after such a remarkable day. Something was not right at the inn and of that he was certain. Walking slowly toward the front desk he questioned Franz if he were alright or had he said or done something that didn't sit well. He could not have known he was in for a harsh lecture.

"You want to know if I'm alright? Nothings wrong with me for your information. It's your damn uncle who's the problem, putting his nose where it don't belong. It's enough already with his obsession about some dead Nazi and by the way, the town's folk say it's interfering in the town business he's supposed to be doing. If I'd been at that meeting in the town hall I'd have said don't drag the good village people into your troubled world. I understand he'll be in my place for dinner tonight so you best tell him to mind his own bloody business."

"Franz, what's he done to get you so worked up? It took a lot of guts to address the town folk, wanting to stem any problems before they began. He's been through an awful lot and life has not been easy. He's exiled from the family farm discovering it was recently destroyed and there's much more. The purpose of the town hall meeting was to relate certain facts about Rudolf Hess and why the village might become a neo-Nazi shrine. To me that's not being nosy but caring."

"He's turned himself into a grand inquisitor, demanding people in the village tell him about their lives between May of 1941 and the end of the war in 1945. He sent out a questionnaire asking very personal questions I and others took great offense to. Greta and I received those forms and did the right thing, tossing them into the fire. Many folks were disconcerted and troubled by his antics. If that's town business because it was written on town stationary, he ought to be run out of town. This is a nice quiet village Mr. McCann and we respect each other's privacy. He was asking very personal questions and frankly I and others don't like this. I don't care if you share this conversation with him but I would ask you to tell him to back off before somebody does something regretful."

"Franz I don't know what to say. If that's the case I need to remind you Hess' presence in this village, albeit a rather short one could have a significant impact, especially now due to his recent death. I don't see's his action as prying but trying to find certain answers to the hours Hess spent in the village. I believe he would like to sit down with you and share what this is all about, especially since you weren't at the meeting. Please don't take it personally." Bah was all Franz managed to say adding "Seven O'clock sharp."

Theo knew why Sander asked the probing questions, obviously searching for clues if anyone knew about a mysterious child wandering about Eaglesham. He'd obviously targeting a select group alive in that troublesome May.

He'd discuss the trouble with Sander hoping to put an end to what Franz called harassment. He hadn't seen the questionnaire but was certain Sander directed it around his theory, had anyone remembered seeing a young child walking around the village. It was obvious Sander had not put Hess or the jacket aside as promised, making his suspicions public with disastrous results. Sander created new problems for himself and suddenly the tiny village was ready to vilify him, led by Franz.

Dinner was promptly served at seven by Franz with no Greta. Theo asked if he might peek into the kitchen and thank her for a wonderful dinner but Franz insisted no. He gestured to Theo to walk outside with him.

"If you want to know the reason why you haven't seen Greta it's because of your uncle's prying. She's very sensitive and doesn't appreciate anyone asking her about her past. Some things are best not disturbed and left buried Mr. McCann and your uncle's questionnaire forced her to think about a very unpleasant time in her life. Leaving the past behind is how she chooses to live and you never know what people have gone through in their lives. Asking personal questions about someone's past can be extremely harmful and she's not alone wanting the past undisturbed. A number of townspeople expressed the same dissolution believing Sander crossed the line from unofficial mayor to using a bully pulpit to pry into people's lives. I'll tell her you enjoyed the meal but don't expect to see her when your uncle's around. Take him back to his lodging if you don't mind because my good customers know he's here and they won't come in until he's gone."

Thinking about Sander Theo's mind flip flopped. Speak forthrightly and convince him to back off or keep the conversation with Franz to himself, a curious thought intertwined in the trouble. Were Franz and Greta being a bit too sensitive about something as seemingly innocuous as few requests for information? Had Sander touched a raw nerve with them or others? He decided not to tell Sander about the confrontation, at least until the morning.

"I'm turning in early," Sander remarked. "It was a very quiet day at the town hall and strangely not a soul came by, something highly unusual. I guess things are running smoothly in the village."

Chapter Thirty Eight

Theo had a fitful night worrying about Sander, vowing to bring up the issue in the least non-threatening manner. He'd be cautious because in a few days he'd be heading home, wanting everything settled to everyone's satisfaction. As to how to use his remaining time in the village, he would help Sander find his own place with no ghosts.

The dark dream was one of the most frightening ever. He dreamed he'd been shot, conscious and knowing that he was about to die. The dream cast a deep pall over the morning.

At breakfast there was disappointment with the cold cereal and dry toast in lieu of Gretchen's famous spread. Not only was Sander on their bad side but by association he and Noah were too. He knew Sander had acted innocently, not realizing his effort would be toxic. Was someone in the village beside Franz and Greta afraid of the past?

The short walk to the town hall felt different, the few townspeople out and about ignoring him, their icy stares different from the usual smiles. Walking into the town hall and Sander's office home he observed papers scattered about the floor and many more piled high on Sander's desk. Others were taped to the wall behind the desk with notations.

"What's going on Sander," said with uneasiness.

"I'm an old man and I'm running out of time is what's going on. I've gotten scores of negative reactions but I don't regret asking. You've been very patient Theo, allowing me to ramble and rant about Hess to the point of it being an obsession. You could easily have said enough you old windbag, I didn't come here for this and I would respect that. Theo I'll cut right to the chase because you've got to be tending to Noah when he returns. I firmly believe in my heart that someone in this village knows what happened that day. What and how much I'm not sure but someone knows. I also think it's possible one or more of them were involved in the life of a young boy. If certain members the royal family held deep sympathies for Hitler and the Nazis, maybe some of the villagers did too. I'm stuck on the idea that at least one person who lived here or still lives here knows about Hess' curious appearance. Why would I think that? Because after years examining countless aspects of Hess' life, that flight jacket has got to have more to it than it appears. Assuming it was a boy on board he could not have disappeared or survived without help. Whether it was the Duke acting as a German agent or someone in the village, someone knows and I'd like to meet that person.

"All this paper work are the responses, some thirty returned. Most are blank, some cursing me in no uncertain terms, almost all anonymous. Someone other than me has to have some knowledge of the hours Hess spent in Eaglesham. From those who responded to my questions, a few said they knew nothing about that day and time. I've looked into the eyes of many villagers over the past weeks to see if anyone bore Hess's deep dark eyes. Theo, I wished to heaven I'd never met the man. Contacting the villagers was probably the wrong thing to do, particularly in Eaglesham where privacy is paramount. We have such genuine care for each other and I've betrayed many.

"Forgive an old man for being a fool Theo. Hess remains a cancer growing out of control and I know it's killing me and in the end it'll probably be the death of me. I'll try to keep this promise Theo. When you fly home with Noah this time know that I'm trying to give up but you know something? If I kill the cancer there's a good chance it'll also kill the patient. I honestly don't have a death wish but I know I've lived in death's shadow for a long time because I once came face to face with one of the most evil and vile men ever to walk this earth. I was this close to the devil. With my remaining days I'll try not to follow anymore hunches or harbor suspicions, even if they smack me in the face. I'm going to try to quit cold turkey. I know you talked with Franz but do you have an idea what other villagers are saying about me?"

"I'm sorry Sander but I hear a lot of grumbling, proving this is a very private and tight knit community. They took offense and whether it was because you touched a raw nerve or because you pried, it really doesn't matter. The closer you get to the fire the hotter it gets and that's why you need to stand down. I'm worried about you Sander. I worry Noah won't be able to visit in the future because you'll have worked yourself into a grave. A famous American inventor who's name I can't recall chose his last earthly words carefully, saying my work is done why wait. Sander should I be concerned about you? Maybe Dr. Joan can offer some helpful advice. Please don't do something rash."

Sander smiled shaking his head, a knowing look on his face in lieu of words. Tears ran down into his white beard. "I hear you Theo. I might be old but I'm planning on sticking around long enough to start another homestead. Physical labor cures all ills and I want to find a place where Noah can visit and feel at home. You can do me one favor though."

"Anything Sander."

"Help me gather up this mess so we can throw these papers into the peat fire. I don't want anything left reminding me of my foolishness."

The morning gratefully passed without further mention of Sander's faux pas or nemesis Hess. The two talked about their ancestors and life on the farm over the centuries. The slow burning peat cast it's usual spell, both men feeling the weight not so heavy on their shoulders for the moment. Theo told Sander the story of falling in love, getting married and raising two young boys in a town very different from Eaglesham,

"The memories live on and though Noah hasn't recovered from the accident, we'll continue to deal with it. He's all I've got Sander, the focus of my life. When we go home I'll do my best to turn our house into a home once again which won't be easy. With luck and hard work I'll make sure Noah gets all the help he needs so he comes out whole and strong. When Dr. Joan and Noah return we'll have a short heartfelt reunion and then I'd love to accompany her to the airport to get a full report about Noah. She's going to have to hustle to make her flight but it'll give us a chance to talk.

Chapter Thirty Nine

Dr. Joan and Noah arrived at the town hall, the boy rushing inside hugging his father and great uncle Sander. Dr. Joan followed, cheeks rosy and hair helter-skelter courtesy of the powerful gale force winds at the loch.

"Mission accomplished she said. When you get the film processed take a good hard look and I think you'll be surprised. Noah is an inquisitive and thoughtful traveling companion and it was a very special time for us both."

When Noah hugged Dr. Joan she mouthed the words, "We're a team you know.'

"I have to run, a plane to catch and a humongous work day tomorrow. I'll have no time for sleep on the plane but that's okay because I've got scores of notes to prepare for my meetings. Noah, I'll see you and your dad when you return in a couple of days but in the meantime remember what I said and keep it close to your heart. I greatly enjoyed your company and I'm very much looking forward to traveling with you one day again in the future."

There were hugs all around and sad smiles. Theo reminded Dr. Joan he'd ride to the airport and catch a ride back to Eaglesham later.

Chapter Forty

When Theo returned from the airport he saw something different in the way Noah carried himself. Sander also seemed more at peace, the winds of change at work due to their closeness. There still was an ever present uneasiness but things felt like they were beginning to turn around. Sander and Noah looked content, a journey to the village toy store for art supplies the highlight of their hours together.

On the ride from the airport Theo suspected the best way to smooth things over would be to have a private talk with Greta. He thought her more reasonable and therefore she might be the catalyst. Sander had crossed the line but it was important the mess be settled before he and Noah took their leave. Walking into the inn he felt a coolness and it wasn't the weather, which was warm for a change.

The inn was also darker than usual, he and Noah having to feel their way past the reception area up the stairs to their room. Theo asked yes and no questions about the boy's time with Sander, beginning with did you have a wonderful time. If it were only possible to utter just one yes or no it would be independence day, cause for celebration.

They ate sandwiches for dinner and strolled about the town after all the shops closed. When darkness fell they returned to the inn, using the last of the peat to warm the room. Theo expected a very cold night lay ahead, guessing there would be no more peat deliveries. I'll be back in a moment he told Noah, needing to have a face to face with Franz to request some peat. No heat and no food had become insufferable. Not unexpected Franz was not at the reception desk. In frustration he rang the bell summoning either Franz or Greta to no avail.

I could pound the reception bell all night he thought, deliberately ignored. Walking back to the staircase he paused, hearing loud knocking at the front door. Maybe it was Franz or Greta or possibly a guest asking for a room. To his great surprise and bewilderment it was Dr. Joan, suitcase in one hand, a large brown bag in the other.

"What happened to your flight" Theo confusedly asked?

"My flight was cancelled because the plane that was to take us back to the states was grounded in New York due to bad weather. We were given vouchers for nearby hotels and one dinner, told to report back to the airport tomorrow at the same time for a seven-thirty evening departure."

"So you decided to make the drive back to Eaglesham and stay here?"

"I did. I cashed in the hotel voucher and used the other to pick up dinner for us. Where's Franz or Greta because I need to secure a room for the night?"

"It's a long sad story and I'll fill you in upstairs but my God, you're going to make a young boy awfully happy. By the way I don't really think you can get a room tonight because Franz and Gretchen are AWOL. Come on up to our room and relax there. We ate cold stale sandwiches for dinner so whatever you brought would be very welcomed. This Mexican standoff between Franz and the McCann's is wearing."

Still no sign of Franz or Greta.

"I'm sorry about your flight delay because I know you needed to get back. Hate to say this but you truly are a saint to think about us and I'm very happy to see you again. As to Noah's time with Sander while I was away, well I hate to curse myself but I have this awareness we might be nearing a breakthrough. You're unexpected appearance might just be what the doctor ordered."

When Noah looked up seeing Dr. Joan his mouth opened and out came squealing of delight followed by a great hug. "I missed you too my Nessie friend" Dr. Joan whispered.

After devouring the sumptuous food Noah got his bedtime story read by Dr. Joan. When he fell asleep Theo suggested the two go downstairs to look for Franz and get a second room. Again there was no response to the reception bell at the front desk. Like thieves in the night they took armfuls of peat from the downstairs fireplace, quickly retreating up the stairs before getting caught.

Not wanting Noah to overhear their conversation if by chance he awoke, Theo put a few bricks of peat into the fire and he and Dr. Joan tiptoed out. They parked themselves on the old sofa near the downstairs fire to stay warm.

"Here's the latest situation. Sander approached a number of townspeople with some rather personal questions about their past lives, especially around the time Hess arrived. He's got a stubborn streak but his intended good intention created a mini firestorm. He wanted to discover if any of the townspeople could somehow have been involved in the life of a young boy, a stranger who might have wandered the village, perhaps even given shelter. His questions bothered a good many folks, some brushing it off but others taking great offense, especially Franz and Greta. The result was not what Sander expected but in truth the questions really did border on an invasion of privacy, not sitting well with most of the townsfolk. Franz was quite insulted and mad as a wet hen. I got an earful from him denouncing Sander as the grand inquisitor, hinting he should give up his town duties and leave everyone alone. Why the unexpected and vitriol response? I have no idea but that's the situation so I doubt we'll see Franz. We've got the largest room in the place and the beds are huge so Noah and I can share one and you'll have your own. Is that alright with you?"

"I accept your offer but before we retire I'd like to learn more about your uncle's troubles, and I don't mean Mr. Hess. Do you want me to talk to him about his obsession?"

"Possibly."

An hour later the downstairs peat fire began to die and it was time to make their way upstairs. Dr. Joan put an extra blanket on Noah, kissing him gently on the cheek. "I'm not sure about your plans for tomorrow but I'd like to use some of my time before I go back to the airport talking with Noah again. I do see some chinks in his armor and perhaps I can create a few more."

In the morning there was still no sign of Franz or Greta, apparently wanting nothing to do with any McCann Theo suspected. A nagging question could not be answered. Why did Franz take such great exception to what was done in innocence?" The reaction totally out of character for someone who'd been kind and helpful. Was he hiding something? Probably not he sensed but the reaction was certainly out of kilter. Poor Sander he rued. Would he become the town pariah, forcing him to become the town's lonely hermit?

Noah and Dr. Joan left on a morning hike, Theo staying behind determined to smooth things over with Franz. There was also the issue of Dr. Joan's overnight stay to take care of. If he could manage to sooth ruffled feathers he'd feel a lot better leaving Sander. At mid morning he spied Greta going out the front door, shopping bags in hand. Deciding to follow staying a fair distance behind, he was uncertain what he might say if he caught up. Observing her stops at the fish and vegetable market he thought about the wonderful meals she'd prepared when things weren't in turmoil. When she began walking back in the direction of the inn Theo approached her. "Can I help carry some of your heavier bags? I'm heading back to the inn myself."

"Very kind of you to offer Mr. McCann but I can manage."

Greta turned her back and walked away but moments later she paused and turned facing Theo.

"My husband is a good and decent man who had a very difficult childhood. There are things in his past that when stirred create misery and depression you or your uncle couldn't understand. I know your uncle didn't intentionally mean to harm anyone, but he did, making Franz nervous, edgy and angry. His past is not so far behind you see and it doesn't take much to reawaken old nightmares. Can I trust you not to repeat what I'd like to share next?"

"Why don't we go inside the coffee shop and I'll tell you the reason why my great uncle sent out the questionnaire. And yes I'll keep whatever you tell me to myself."

Theo spoke first, describing Sander's difficult life since the day Rudolf Hess crash landed on his farm. He described the travails that followed and how forty years later they continued haunting him. He didn't want to delve too deep into Sander's life so he left it at that. Greta listened without comment, occasionally shaking her head or grimacing at Sander's misfortunes over the years.

"So you see Greta, life had not been easy for my uncle. His obsession with Hess is a disease, eating him up and tormenting him most of his adult life. He hasn't been able to enjoy the good life, constantly looking over his shoulder for fear of what he might see or hear. I'm not apologizing for Sander but I know he wasn't out to hurt anyone. He's a good proud man who unfortunately found himself in the right place at the wrong time, forever linked to one of the most evil person who ever lived."

"I'm terribly sorry for your uncle and I hope he finds peace. I've known him a very long time and had no idea the burden he carried. If you've got a little more time there is something you might want to know about the burdens we carry.

"My loving husband Franz was born in Germany, using wile and deception to avoid most of the horrors and atrocities of the Nazi regime. He was orphaned at a very early age, forced to live by his wits, wandering the bombed out cities of Germany scavenging through wreckage for scraps of food.

"It's a miracle he survived, walking for months and months across the troubled country until finally crossing the border into Holland. Sadly he was not welcomed because of what the Germans did to their country during the war. He traveled by foot to Rotterdam and became a stowaway on a freighter who's destination he did not know. He didn't care where it went as long as it wasn't Germany, hopefully a place where he might begin a new life.

"He hid in the belly of the ship for seven days, tiptoeing around during the night in search of scraps of food. One night he was nearly caught which would have meant returning to Germany. The ship sailed to of all places Scotland to unload cargo. During the noisy and confusing process he snuck away, eventually making his way to Glasgow, finding work as a bag boy at a small hotel. That was the start of his new life and it was there I met Franz. He was part handyman, part cook and gofer. I worked the front desk. Eventually we fell in love, married and saved every bit of money hoping one day we might find an old inn in disrepair we could afford and fix up. Fate brought us to Eaglesham. Nobody in the village knows anything about Franz's difficult childhood so you can imagine how frightening it was to have someone ask questions about his early life. The story the villagers know is that one day while trekking he fell and injured himself, rehabilitating at the inn that we eventually bought. That's the truth. He fell in love with the village, a place where privacy was well protected meaning he felt very safe here."

"I'm very sorry life was so precarious and frightening for Franz when he was a youngster" Theo replied. "Please believe me when I tell you Sander meant no harm to him or anyone. I'm going to tell you Sander's motives but this is strictly between you and me. What's driven Sander these past many years is Rudolf Hess, a sworn member of the German Nazi party who's bad luck caused him to crash land on Sander's farm. The story gets very complicated after that accidental meeting.

"Sander has come to believe there was a passenger on Hess' flight to Scotland, somebody possibly around the age of ten or twelve at the time. Why does he think that? Because he spent time with Hess before his arrest, offering help to a forlorn figure. By the way he did not know he was talking to Adolf Hitler's number two man at the time. He'd been given a false name. When they parted Hess gave Sander a gift, possibly an act of appreciation for agreeing to help him finish his mission. Hess insisted he needed to speak with the Duke of Hamilton as soon as possible and he needed Sander's help.

"The gift? He handed Sander a German flight jacket my uncle believed was the one Hess wore on his flight. Many years later he was shocked discovering it was a child's size jacket, certainly not Hess'. There's never been a hint or even a suggestion in any history book that Hess traveled with a child, but that jacket suggests otherwise. He wanted to ask the townsfolk if anyone was aware of the appearance of a lonely wayward waif.

"The jacket was hidden away in Sander's place for more than forty years and it's still with him today. When all was said and written about Hess' mysterious life I should tell you there was absolutely no mention of a passenger. Franz wasn't the only person Sander approached asking if anyone in the village might have seen a child wandering in 1941. I believe he also harbors the suspicion that little boy could be an adult living in Eaglesham today. If he found him or if he could find out what happened to him, it would finally put Sander's mind and life to rest. You don't have to tell me but since you've told me about Franz is there a story about you?"

"I Like Franz am also an orphan, adopted by a kindly family in Glasgow. I didn't face the kinds of horrors Franz experienced because I was loved and well taken care of. Also I don't have any memory of my childhood in Germany. Mr. McCann I need to get back to the inn so may I ask a huge favor?"

"Of course, anything. If you want me to tell Sander he's looking in the wrong place and back off I will."

"No I simply wish you forget our conversation and when you and your son go home please leave this behind. I know you care very much for your uncle so I hope Franz will get past this. Are we alright with that?"

Chapter Forty One

Theo had no reason to doubt Greta's tale. Americans didn't fully understand the insanity and fear cast by Hitler he understood because they hadn't lived through it. There was a huge difference between reading about lost souls and tragedy in Germany than those who were actually living there. When they said their goodbyes Theo had an inkling that Sander's inflammatory questionnaire might not be the end of his efforts trying to locate anyone who might have known about Hess in Eaglesham. Should he betray Greta revealing what he'd been told? Would that settle the issue that Franz was not a suspect? Probably not he decided and it was against his nature to break promises. Would he consider telling Sander he'd had a long talk with Greta about the situation? At the right time yes but not now. There still might be more to Greta's story he considered.

Franz as a young boy, a castaway on a ship was on his mind. Was it coincidence she'd used the term stowaway? Sander referred to a young visitor in his questionnaire although he couldn't remember the exact wording.

Had Noah and Dr. Joan returned from their adventure? He doubted it so it might be a good time to close his eyes for five minutes he thought. Walking up stairs not paying attention he nearly collided with Franz who was on his way down. Neither acknowledged the other, stepping aside so each could pass. Before Theo reached the top step he turned rather abruptly shouting wait. Franz froze.

"Could we please talk for a few minutes? I'm certain you've got work to do but I'd like to try to make everything right between you and Sander. To tell you the truth….."

Theo was cut off mid sentence, Franz never turning to face him. "You're an outsider Mr. McCann and you wouldn't understand the bond holding us together in this very private hamlet. More than one villager took offense and that was their right. Many my age lived their lives in terror during World War Two, something you Americans don't understand. Us old timers prefer to keep those deep scars tamped way deep down because you see, some wounds never heal. I and others considered his action to be a personal affront but if you're looking for how to deal with this, tell him to go back to tending to town business and forgetting his ridiculous obsession. I think we'll all be okay and this could blow over in time but an apology would be nice. By the way when can I expect you and the boy and that woman checking out?"

"Dr. Ark is leaving this afternoon and Noah and I are possibly leaving tomorrow. I'm very sorry you felt trespassed but I hope for your and Sander's sake you can get past it."

Continuing up the staircase he heard the sound of the front door open accompanied by laughter. It was Noah and Dr. Joan.

Leftovers from the precious night's dinner made a welcomed snack, Dr. Joan explaining they'd lazily meandered country trails without getting lost.

When it was time for Dr. Joan to return to the airport she told Noah she'd see him back at the institute very soon. "Theo when you drop Noah off there come knock on my door because there are things about today I'd like to share. Nothing earth shattering so don't hold your breath because it can wait. Think of it as a report card showing how we're doing and how far we've come."

"Shall we all go over to Uncle Sander's place Noah when Dr. Joan leaves?" Noah nodded grabbing hold of her hand walking her to the car.

There were hugs all around and a batch of new drawings to take home. The rest of the art would find space on Sander's back wall, the new art gallery in town Sander crowed.

"Noah we're staying tonight and most likely tomorrow night and then we'll make our way to Glasgow. From there it's a day afternoon flight home. I'd like to spend a little time with your uncle so why don't you go up to our room and use your new art kit? I'll just be over in the town hall so come by if you get bored." Theo was thankful leaving Noah was manageable.

"There are a few things I want talk over with you Sander. Do you have some time?"

"No time like right now" Sander replied. "What's up?"

"First a story so please take it for what it's worth." There was still time to change his mind he hoped.

"I had a nice long chat with Greta and I'd like to tell you about it because it might put to rest some of your thoughts about the passenger. Greta told me a heartrending story and the bottom line is Franz is not your man. I truly believe you had him in your mind all the time and I won't argue that with you. Franz was born in Germany and would be the right age to be Hess' passenger but trust me. It's not him.

"According to Greta, Franz emigrated to Scotland not on Hess' airplane but by tramp steamer. He'd fled Nazi Germany on foot, eventually stowing away on a cargo ship bound for Scotland. Do I believe Greta? Yes so do yourself a favor. Put this behind you and back off any further intrusions into the lives of the people of this village. The real story if there is one is probably out there and as I've said a few times it's a big world. The path you're on is slippery and I'd hate to see you get hurt. Leave the past alone because some things are never meant to fit together like a large jigsaw puzzle. Don't think for a moment I haven't respected you and your work but for your own sake consider the Hess situation over. Before any more damage is done put it all behind you and live in the now.

"You've got to get along with your neighbors including Franz and the others who took a dim view of your methods. Franz had a frightful childhood but managed to survive relying on wits on his own. Be civil with the man even if he turns his back. One more thing. Come back to the inn with us and share a meal with Noah and me tonight. Put Hess aside and be the good neighbor and the town's caretaker you've always been."

Chapter Forty Two

When and Sander sat down at the table in the inn Theo excused himself to wash up. Instead of going down the hallway to the right he turned left toward Franz's office to speak with him again. Opening the door caused Franz to jump and hastily removing something from his desk cramming it haphazardly into the top drawer. The look of surprise quickly took on a look of irritation.

"I apologize for barging in but I wanted you to know I brought my uncle here for a late lunch. I'd very much like you to both bury the hatchet and now is a good time. Nobody likes someone snooping into their lives so I wholeheartedly understand your reaction. However, in my heart I know my uncle would never deliberately hurt anyone so would you do me a great favor and sit down with us for a few minutes. I'd also like you to ask Greta if she'd make lunch for us."

Franz continued shuffling things from his desk into the drawer, saying he needed a moment. "Do you want your son to hear what we might say to each other? It might not be pretty."

"Probably not so I'll ask him to use the rest room and wash up. If you and Sander can't shake hands in the first five minutes I'm afraid the animosity will never go away."

Franz said he'd be out shortly needing to finish work he was behind on. "Why don't you give me five or ten minutes and in the meantime I'll let Greta know she needs to prepare lunch."

Theo took his leave returning to the table feeling encouraged. When he heard Franz's office door open and close he asked Noah to go down the hall and wash up, taking time to do a good job. "Walk down that hall and turn left. You'll see the door to the bathroom and you'll have to turn the light switch on. Make sure you scrub your fingernails and turn off the light when you leave."

Noah and Franz passed each other like two ships in the night, Noah refusing to acknowledge Franz because of something he'd overheard. Franz had done something bad to Sander he believed. Looking down at his hands to be certain he knew left from right Noah turned right into what he assumed was the bathroom. It was terribly dark, taking a few minutes to feel around for the light switch. To his consternation and confusion when the light went on there was no wash basin or toilet, just a large desk and lamp and photographs on the walls. Walking about to see if one of the many doors in the room led to the bathroom all were locked but one. That one contained coat hooks but no bathroom.

He thought his dad must have said left instead of right so the only thing to do he reckoned was to turn out the light and leave before he got caught. He'd then continue down the hall looking for the restroom making up for his mistake. In the confusion he'd turned out the light, forgetting which door exited to the hallway. Feeling around in the dark he grew anxious and uncertain how to get out. Turning the light on again was not happening because he couldn't find the switch. Feeling around for the desk so he wouldn't bang into it he felt the base of the lamp he'd seen. Grasping hold of the pull chain something heavy fell from the desk to the floor creating a loud bang. Flailing about for the lamp again he grabbed the chain. The sudden burst of light temporarily blinded him, feeling about for the object he'd knocked from the desk in order to put it back.

When his eyes focused he saw the object, a loud gasp and recoil his reaction. It was all too obvious it was a large brown pistol with a long black barrel. How many times had his dad lectured about the dangers of being around a firearm. Scrambling to get as far away as possible he hoped he wouldn't get caught before he found his way out. Alone and frightened he ran about looking for the right exit door. Mercifully it was found and wasting no time he ran down the hall, slowing only at the entrance to the dining area.

"Whoa" Theo shouted. "What's the rush? Lunch hasn't even been ordered yet." It was obvious there was a look of bewilderment on the boy's face.

"What's the matter Noah" Theo said. The wild look in Noah's normally blank eyes couldn't be missed. Running to Sander, Noah clutched him tightly nearly knocking him from his chair.

Sander laughed saying the boy probably needed help in the bathroom, one probably very much different than his in the states. "Maybe seeing the bidet confused him" he told Theo with a wink. "I'll take him and give him a quick tour."

Theo thought the words if the boy could only talk. "Franz, It's quite sad."

Half running and stumbling Noah pulled Sander down the hallway to the room he'd mistakenly entered. Sander cried what's wrong several times, half expecting a response.

Noah pointed to the gun laying on the floor. Sander saw the problem getting down on all fours to take a closer look.

"Noah my boy you did the right thing by getting me and I'm very thankful you didn't try to pick it up. No telling what could have happened. I wonder why it's on the floor."

Noah gasped, pointing to the spot on the desk where it had rested. "Leave it where it is and lets go back to the table acting like everything is normal." Noah nodded.

Returning to the table Sander announced with a knowing smile, "Noah had a little problem finding the soap and towel but once located the boy washed up nicely. Theo could I talk to you alone for a few moments?

There's something you need to know before you go home and I might forget it later."

Theo excused himself, an irritated look on Franz's face suggesting why the need to discuss something in private.

Sander pulled Theo down the hall so they could both eye the pistol on the floor. Sander whispered it was old German Luger, what some gun folks referred to as Pistole Parabellum. "It's an older model. a toggle-locked recoil-operated semi-automatic pistol produced in German between the years1898 and 1948. How do I know? When Mr. Hess gathered up the objects in his survival bag scattered about he cried he couldn't find the Luger, describing it using the words I just uttered. I know for a fact he never found it so what happened to it and how did it get here? What are the chances this one belonged to Hess? I don't believe the Brits found it but I knew they were looking very carefully. It's a long shot but what if that pistol actually once belonged to Hess? I've done a fair amount of shooting with friends in the village and not one of them owned a Luger. Rifles yes but nothing like that."

Franz suspecting something was amiss and upset having to sit with Noah said aloud he was going to find out what Sander and Theo were up to. He walked down the hallway toward his office, seeing the two standing in his private office. Trying to see what they were looking at he realized his weapon was on the floor.

"What the hell are you doing here? Get out right now and then get the hell out of my inn. Mr. Theo McCann you've got five minutes to pack up yout stuff and get out. You Sander McCann, I never want to see you in my inn ever again. That gun you're admiring has great value to me and one of you, most likely Sander was planning on stealing it. It was a wedding gift from Greta many years ago, something I treasure quite highly. Why is it laying on the floor? Did you or your little bastard idiot son have something to do with this?"

Theo lunged but before he could reach Franz he tripped over a chair ending up on the floor. When he looked up Franz was holding the gun standing over Theo's outstretched body. Cocking the trigger he hissed "you and your family have created a great deal of trouble for me and I want you both to know it would be no problem shooting you for trespassing."

Franz took dead aim at Theo's forehead, an angry look on his face. Out of the blue Noah ran toward Franz screaming the word NO. Everyone froze, stunned looks on faces. Sander seized the moment grabbing Franz with his muscular arms. During the struggle the gun fell to the floor. Before Theo could pick it up Greta rushed in and seeing Theo reaching for it she kicked in into the corner. Picking it up she took aim at Theo.

"Unhand my husband because if you don't I'll shoot Sander first and then you and your son."

"Greta" Theo shouted. "We can deal with this. I promise Sander will let go of Franz but you have to allow Noah to leave the room unharmed."

In the midst of the danger Theo froze, suddenly realizing the boy had really shouted the word no. Pulling himself up he ran across the room to cradle Noah. With tears running down his cheeks oblivious to the danger he uttered the words "you actually spoke." In that brief moment everyone simply stared, Greta with the gun still pointing at Sander.

"Theo and Noah have nothing to do with what's going on. This is between you and me and Franz" Sander said calmly. "Please allow them to leave so they can pack their things and be off. I'm responsible for creating trouble in your lives and if you'll allow I can explain everything.

Greta motioned her head toward the door ordering father and son to leave. "If you're not packed and out of our inn in the next ten minutes I'll have no choice but to silence your uncle forever. His snooping has created a unique and troublesome problem for Franz and me."

Theo started to argue but Sander interrupted, saying do what the lady asks. "Theo this isn't your problem and if you do what Greta insists I'm certain we'll get through this. This is between me and Franz and Greta so please go."

CHAPTER FORTY THREE

Theo's single concern was getting Noah out of the inn to a safe place. Sander's town hall office was the only option because there was really nowhere else to go.

"Noah don't worry because your Uncle Sander will be alright" Theo said calmly. "It's a very long story so just believe Sander will not be harmed and we'll all be together shortly. Calmer heads will prevail and the problems will be solved. The big thing is not to worry because nobody's going to hurt your uncle."

Theo knelt down looking Noah directly in the eyes. With righteous reverence he whispered, "you actually spoke." Tears and laughter stymied the other things he wanted to say, repeating over and over you actually spoke. "Can you tell me what you're feeling right now?"

Looking lost and confused a sheepish smile preceded what Theo had waited a long relentless time to hear; Noah's sweet voice. Unable to say another word though Noah sobbed until his tiny body shook. "Sander" he said, a look of incredulity on Theo's face. "Don't you worry Uncle Sander can take care of himself. You might not understand this but he's a tough old bird." He was right Noah had no idea what that meant but it was funny and the boy laughed away the tears. "He'll be coming back to this office very soon so we just have to sit tight and wait."

Theo tried not to think about a gun shot he might hear. In the quiet of the closed up town hall every little sound unhinged him, the hardest part not being there to stand up for Sander. If there ever was a time to wear a calm demeanor he prayed it was then.

Would Sander actually saunter into the room with the situation resolved Theo wondered? Did Greta or Franz feel they had to resort to murder to possibly save themselves? Had Sander by accident struck an extremely sensitive and vulnerable part of their lives?

Minutes passed, the town hall so quiet he and Noah heard the sounds of mice scurrying about. Theo desperately wanted to look out the front door but he couldn't leave Noah or expose himself to danger. He realized there was little to nothing he might do.

The first half hour passed with no sound of gunfire nor the sight of Sander. If I go back into the inn he wondered, would that put Sander in more danger or might I save him? Another fifteen minutes passed in absolute silence, Theo's mouth so dry he couldn't form words, a taste of Noah's silent world.

What sounded like a gunshot caused Theo to drop to his knees, pulling Noah down to protect him, trying mightily to stifle a scream in his throat. The sound reverberated around the empty reception area of the town hall, followed frightfully by the sound of footfalls. Someone was in the town hall, possibly coming for them.

With heart pounding in terror Theo tried to convince himself the gunshot was an accident and Sander was unharmed. When his head cleared a bit he sensed it was not a gunshot but someone slamming the large heavy front door shut. Sander used to scold the townspeople for slamming the front door all the time. But if the footfalls were not his, was Franz or Greta coming for them?

The foot falls stopped near the reception desk outside the doorway to Sander's home-office. A loud knock caused he and Noah to jump. Placing all his weight on Noah with one hand covering the boy's eyes, he looked about for place to hide him. In a flash it came to him, remembering the dark corner where Sander had stashed the flight jacket. Hearing a voice outside the locked door the words were too garbled to understand. Another menacing knock felt ominous, creating more fear and great sadness.

Putting an ear to the door he heard heavy labored breathing, expecting the door to be broken down. He tried to recall if there was an escape path for he and Noah because whoever was at the door was not going away quietly. He suddenly remembered something Sander once described. Behind the dark recess in the office was a hidden doorway leading to the old bell tower staircase. He could hide Noah there he realized, telling him to climb the stairs and shout out to any passing townsperson below for help. He hustled Noah to the stairs and looked about for something that might block the doorway.

In the time it took to get Noah onto the stairs he realized it was suddenly very quiet near the door. Had the person given up and gone away? His hope was dashed when he heard a key in the lock, the spare key Sander left in the reception desk top drawer. He whispered "Noah don't make a sound." The door to Sander's office slowly opened, making a sound as if someone were scratching fingernails on a blackboard.

Swallowing the bile in his throat he expected the worst. To his utter amazement when the door fully opened there was Sander.

Chapter Forty Four

Theo's first tentative words were are you okay, his mind in turmoil, his body paralyzed. For several moments he was torn between joy seeing him and the panic that held him tight. When able to think clearly he remembered Noah saying that one word. Without prompting Noah appeared asking, "Uncle Sander are you really alright?"

Theo and Noah wore looks on their face saying they'd just seen a ghost. Sander told Noah those words were the most beautiful sounds he'd ever heard. The reality that the long dark winter might be over was nearly too overwhelming to grasp. Soon everyone found themselves laughing without end.

"Well" Noah uttered, to gales of more laughter?

"Indeed I am very well son and boy do I have a whale of a tale to tell. Let's get a peat fire going first and then I'll tell the most amazing story, courtesy of Franz and Greta. When the flames warmed the room Sander began..

"Franz and Greta have actually been holding onto a secret between themselves ever since they first stepped foot in the village. Thanks to their candor one troubling riddle has truly been solved. Theo I say this sincerely I promise Rudolf Hess will no longer be a part of my life. By the way you still have your room at the inn so stay as long as you can, gratis. Sitting back with eyes closed Sander held sway once again.

The only one talking was Noah repeating Dr. Joan promised he'd be able to talk one day,

"Thank you Uncle Sander for telling all those stories that I really enjoyed. You and Dr. Joan and Dad helped me a lot." Theo reflected on all the pains they'd gone through but he'd think about that another day and another time. He'd paid a huge price but it was so worth the cost.

"I've said this before and maybe it's the last time I'll use this corny American expression, but fasten you seatbelts."

"Ah me where to start" Sander mused. "It actually might be better to start at the end and work back to the beginning. The first thing I want to say is that the small flight jacket has finally been returned to it's original owner."

"Sander after Franz had his a meltdown I kind of suspected he was that little boy so many years ago in Hess' plane. Is that what you learned?"

"Don't interrupt. I'm just getting started. Greta painstakingly related the tale about Franz wandering alone, using his wiliness and guile to escape the Nazi horrors in German as a young boy. She bared her soul emphasizing Franz was an orphan just like her, doing what ever he could to stay alive one more day. His goal was to walk out of Nazi Germany and live in peace. I need to make this point very clear. He did not leave Germany in a plane. The truth is he walked across the border into Holland and later boarded a ship unbeknownst to him sailing to Scotland. She called the young Franz brave and crafty and honest. Greta broke down several time describing his heroic fight to survive. I wondered why Franz was not telling his story but from the look on his face, I believe he was too overcome by Greta's emotional saga.

"Franz arrived in Scotland all alone Theo via the sea and that proved he was not the passenger with Hess. Actually I thought those were the words I'd heard. If he was not, well at that point I realized it could be anyone, anywhere in the world about that age. Did the jacket belong to a child chosen by Hess to accompany him?"

One of Sander's well known quirks was to pause when his story was preparing to make a sudden shift. Theo had seen that many times before, usually when Sander stopped talking to tamp tobacco down into his pipe. This time he took extra long time to light it just right. When the first plume of smoke reached the rafters he announced he was told something quite remarkable. Noah who usually kept to himself when the adults talked moved closer to Sander.

"Here's where it gets interesting Theo and you too Noah. So the passenger definitely was not Franz but thanks to Greta, she confirmed that there was passenger and the passenger was not a stowaway. When Hess took flight that May day in 1941, Franz was marching through the German countryside thinking about the Dutch forests somewhere ahead. As an aside I heard the most remarkable tale of what it took to stay alive another day. Franz knew the name Hess as did most Germans. He even once attended a Hitler rally when Rudolf Hess gave a fiery introductory speech. He'd only learned about Hess' flight long after he met Greta.

"No it was not Franz so Greta reminded me probing into certain people's lives often brings unexpected harm.

"If you're curious about the Luger Greta put it down relating something I promised never to reveal to another living soul. It hurts me to betray her but you and Noah were witnesses to what happened in Franz's office. I agreed and that's when we sat down and I heard a most heartrending and remarkable tale.

"The jacket? Believe it or not it belonged to Greta. She flew with Hess although she admitted she did not know who he was or where they were going. I found her story quite remarkable, buoyed by the thought I hadn't been chasing invisible gremlins all these past weeks and months. Greta was also an orphan and here's her story.

"She said she never knew her real parents, growing up in isolated village in the beautiful Bavarian Alps. She attended school there, very much a commune. Later she learned it was an orphanage for children of Germans and Austrian lineage born to parents none ever knew. Life was generally good she insisted, the worst part the ongoing physical exams, blood tests and probing and poking plus too many silly word games. She knew nothing about the outside world while there, sheltered and unaware there were troubles in Germany or even that a war was happening.

"One day she and two others, a boy and a girl were summoned to the medical building and put through a rigorous series of tests. At the completion the boy and girl were dismissed but she was told to stay. From that day on she was separated from the other children, never told why changes in her routines. Exhausting weeks of agility tests, many very painful were endured. Shooting practice and English language studies were a scheduled part of her day.

"At the end of the training she said a uniformed man came to the school spending time talking with her. He said he was taking her out of school so that she could perform a heroic act for the German nation. Discipline was very important at the orphanage including never questioning authority. There were stern lectures about Nordic folk lore and the German theory of racial superiority she was forced to memorize. The unformed man asked questions she didn't understand but he seemed pleased with the answers she gave. Greta was eleven years old at the time and unbeknownst to her, she was about to embark on a journey altering her life forever.

"The uniformed man she learned much later was Rudolf Hess. History will prove that he'd been given access to the records of all the children at the orphanage, including the names of their biological fathers but not their mothers. Long after the flight and grown up and married to Franz, she read about something called Project Thor. It disturbed her realizing that she was one of it's prized children, kept in the dark about who her biological father was. Hess promised he would tell her at the end of their special mission. After Hess' engine sputtered there were no more words, describing the agitation and cursing done by the pilot, screaming bad luck.

"He ordered her to put on her parachute, something she'd practiced repeatedly. His last words are permanently etched in her mind. 'A new world is being created and you are blessed because you have a very important man's blood flowing through your veins.'

"The plane began shaking terribly she recalled, nosing down out of control. The pilot unbuckled himself she said, reaching across the cabin to open the door on her side. Whatever happens you will be alright he shouted over the sound of the rushing wind. Someone is waiting for you and he will take good care of you. He unbuckled her seatbelt, removed the parachute cover and pushed her out the door. When she looked up the plane was gone and above her a tiny parachute was carrying her over the countryside.

"The moment she hit the ground she said two men on horses rode toward her, saying not a word, just gathering her up and undoing her harness. They rode through the forest to a place she perceived to be a palace.

"She lived there for a week until one day a man and a woman came for her, soon to become her foster parents. Unfortunately this is where her recollections begin to fade. Most likely the palace was the Duke's estate and if that's true, he was certainly not the loyal Brit people believed. Greta swore she did not know the pilot was Hess and as she was taught she did not ask. When tossed from the plane she thought it was the end of her earthly life. Greta never saw the man again and didn't discover it was Rudolf Hess until the Nuremburg trials when his face appeared in news reels.

"She'd removed her flight jacket on the plane because the heat was stifling she told me. I assume Hess found it in the wreckage and gave it to me rather than have the Brits find it. I always knew if I found the person it was intended for or who it belonged to I was going to return it. That person is Greta. As to who her real biological father was sadly she'll never know. Was the pilot her father? She could not or would not answer.

"You know the rest of her story how she and Franz worked together at a hotel in Glasgow, later falling in love and marrying. The trekking bringing them eventually to Eaglesham was purely coincidental and had nothing to do with Hess. She was actually quite surprised when she learned that she'd come full circle in her life, parachuting into a village where one day she would live.

"Franz learned her remarkable story several years into their marriage, taking it upon himself to locate Greta's real parents if they were alive. If there were records they'd been destroyed by the Nazi's during the closing days of the war he discovered. The Luger? Greta discovered it on the ground in the clearing where she landed, assuming it fell from the plane when she was pushed out. Conjecture, assumptions, fate, maybe all three to her story but certainly a great element of truth. One final thought. You can't repeat a word of anything I've just said. It would create a media storm and those poor people would have their lives picked apart.

"There you have it, reminding me a bit of one of your novels Theo. I might have to re-read it in my new free time, something I am going to cherish. There actually might be a story in all this for your next book, with names and settings changed of course so it could not be traced to Eaglesham. Think about it."

"Sander you can now let go of Rudolf Hess and spend your remaining years doing things that you used to love. You were right all along about a second passenger but it's quite interesting that only you, Franz, Greta, Noah and I will ever know about that."

"Franz and Greta will never go to the authorities with their story and I promised I wouldn't either. Theo, it really would make wonderful historical fiction, with an emphasis on the fiction of course.

"I now understand the dread and panic Franz felt when I started asking questions about the time Hess came to earth in Eaglesham. I wouldn't have heard this story if it weren't for you being here with me. Thank you for all you've done and you Noah, you and I will always be in each other's hearts. There's a lot more to the Hess' story but I'll leave that to others. Fate? chance? Obsession? When this all sinks in perhaps it isn't the amazing discoveries we made, but how one defining shout from Noah changed the world."

"Before we go home I want Noah to call Dr. Joan Theo announced. She of course would not recognize the voice so he'll certainly have fun with her. She'd always insisted it would happen one day but no one could have expected it under these strange circumstances.

"What are you going to do now Sander with your new found freedom and peace? Other mysteries connected to Hess will entice but I hope you'll allow others to deal with them. Do you have it in you to start another farm?"

"Maybe but not in the foreseeable future. I haven't been out of the village of Eaglesham since the day Hess fell to earth so I'd very much like to do some traveling. One of these days I'd like Noah to return, you too of course so he can point out where he saw Nessie. Can you imagine a Scotsman living all his life here and never looking for the Loch Ness Monster?

"As long as they'll have me I'll continue to do my duties managing the village. The fight as always is stopping the hectic modern world from infringing. If someone who'd lived here a hundred years ago came back, he or she would see very little had changed. I know I can't rebuild the old homestead but eventually I'd like to find a small home. What about you?"

"Noah and I have a lot of hard work in front of us. The accident tragedy cut deeply and it'll take time and lots of help to repair all the damage. I have Noah back and you know what? For a long time I felt like I'd lost both sons. I might even ask Dr, Joan if she'd want to join Noah on certain special occasions, such as his birthday in a few weeks or a return visit with you Sander. I know her work life is about to change but I know she'll always be nearby. It's a bittersweet story.

"Why don't we meet at the inn tonight at seven this time with all the craziness behind us. We'll have a fitting farewell dinner and I'd like to ask Franz and Greta to join us. Okay with you?"

"Please Uncle Sander," Noah chimed in.

"Only if after dinner you and I go out and search not for butterflies, but the beautiful Scottish lightening bugs. Bet you've never seen one. Deal?"

"Deal."

When Theo settled into his home with his chatty son he began work on a new suspense novel about a lost boy. He had a most difficult time starting the story, hours staring at a blank page knowing there was much to say. After much deliberation he jumped to the epilogue, knowing what he would write. It would be the dedication, the words to Noah, my darling young son.

The End

Epilogue

Theo, Dr. Joan, Noah, Sander, Fritz and Greta are fictional characters. Rudolf Hess was a German Nazi so much in tune with Adolf Hitler he could execute his will without being commanded.

Hess was once named heir to his Fuhrer, Hitler's first deputy. Given that position he was privy to much of Hitler's scheming and planning, including how to conduct war and the planning and carrying out of the Final Solution. He was a brawler by nature, a good soldier as long as Hitler kept him on a short leash.

Hess feared a two prong war; on the eastern front against the enormous Soviet Empire, in the west against the steadfast Island of Great Britain. While the blitz was destroying many cities in England and Scotland, Hitler believed England would surrender soon so he violated the peace accord with the Soviets, assigning his generals the task of invading and conquering the entire Soviet Union.

There were some stark difference of opinion between Hess and Hitler how to manage the war, Hess usually totally subservient to the Fuhrer. Hess managed his duties to the Nazi Party until a great rift developed that could not be gulfed.

When Hess learned of Hitler's planned surprise attack (Operation Barbarossa) against the Soviet Union, he feared for the future of Germany. A two prong war was reason for the defeat of Germany in World War One. Hess feared history would repeat itself.

Known only to a few close conspirators, Hess secretly began devising a plan to end hostilities between England and Germany, thus allowing troops on the Eastern front the tools necessary to subdue the Soviet Union. When secret negotiations between Hess and a high ranking Englishman failed to produce any interest in peace between Germany and England, Hess decided a more direct approach would have to be taken. He wrote his son Wolfe emphasizing there are higher powers than you might find in the highest offices in the land. I am talking about more fateful powers he would write, the diving powers which intervene in time when great events will occur.

The man chosen to receive Hess's offer of a solid peace between the two nations was a prominent Scotsman, the Duke of Hamilton. His first letter to the Duke suggested a meeting in a neutral city, perhaps Lisbon. The Duke did not respond.

With the Soviet Union in Hitler's sights, deputy Rudolf Hess became more and more anxious to engineer a peace settlement with England. When all seemed futile an idea arose. In early December of 1940 he asked to have a special Messerschmitt 110 aircraft designed and built for his own personal use. It was to be a twin engine fighter-bomber modified for long distance flying. Ordinarily the plane carried two men but it could easily be flown solo with modifications. When questioned about the private plane, Hess said he was privileged because he was after all, Hitler's deputy.

He kept his plane at the Augusburg airfield and flew often to get used to the instruments. No one questioned his flights, at least not openly. Each day he requested his secretary get the latest aviation weather forecasts for the British Isles. A map of Scotland was procured and mounted on the wall of his bedroom. In time he memorized all the prominent features of the terrain.

On April 30 Hitler's birthday Hess prepared to make a flight to Scotland. He was in his plane, engines running, waiting for permission to take off when one of his adjutants approached holding an envelope. It was an order from Hitler asking Hess to stand in for him the next day, May 1 at the

Messerschmitt Works to award medals to a few officers. He climbed down from the cockpit to prepare his remarks. dejected as the weather was ideal. The Fuhrer was everything to him, often saying it was a rare privilege to serve such a man and to follow his ideas with such success.

With the imminent invasion of the Soviet Union on the near horizon, Hess set May 10th as his departure date. On that date he took off from the airport, flying west toward the Duke of Hamilton's estate near Eaglesham, some fifteen miles from Glasgow.

When an envelope containing a message for Hitler was opened after the successful takeoff, high officials in Germany gathered to figure out how to deal with Hess.

In an official statement Goebbels depicted Hess as an ailing man under the influence of mesmerists and astrologers. A high ranking Nazi official declared he was an everlasting idealist and a very sick man. In short order those accused of abetting Hess were arrested and taken to concentration camps. Willy Messerschmitt was summoned to defend himself after being accused of being an accomplish. How could you allow someone as obviously insane as Hess to have an airplane he was asked. His reply added insult to injury. He supposedly said am I supposed to believe that a lunatic can hold such a high office in the Third Reich.

In truth many persons associated with Hess swore he showed no ordinary signs of insanity. Rumors ran rampant. Had the German's sent a rather clever double others believed. Was Hess an assassin who's true mission was to get as close to Churchill as possible and poke him with a poison ring?

Goring insisted the Luftwaffe scramble into the air and intercept the wayward pilot. Word went out the deputy Fuhrer had gone mad. He must be brought down Goring insisted. Goring was beside himself, even though his aides insisted he did not have enough fuel to reach his intended landing site, saying the RAF would shoot him down. Goring was assured that it was unlikely Hess would survive the flight.

Crossing the Scottish border, Hess descended from twelve thousand feet before beginning a rapid descent. Several Scotsmen reported a German plane flew as low as fifty feet above the earth. To RAF authorities it all seemed too improbable. Nearing Glasgow radar indicated the plane was flying at three hundred miles an hour. Hess exited the country's west coast of the Firth of Clyde, then turned around and flew back over the mainland.

Soaring over Scotland Hess realized he was nearly out of fuel, having only a vague idea where he was. He flew at six thousand feet looking for familiar landmarks and a clearing where he might have to land. When the engine sputtered he decided to bail out. He shut off the engines and opened the cockpit. The rushing air pinned him to his seat until he remembered a lesson he's been taught. Roll the plane he told himself, let gravity free him. When he fell from the cockpit his left foot struck the plane's twin tails.

A ground observer in Eaglesham reported that an aircraft had crashed and the pilot bailed out appearing to have landed safely. A plowman found him, taking him to his cottage where the pilot was offered tea. When police arrived, Hess calling himself Albert Horn was taken to a local police station. His only words were he expected to be treated well, like British airmen of high rank who fell from the sky in Germany.

He was briefly interrogated, stating he was okay, was in no trouble and had flown deliberately with a vital message for the Duke of Hamilton. Hess said he wanted to land on the Duke's property, producing a map with the location of the Dungavel House clearly marked.

It took several hours before it was determined it was not Captain Horn, but the number one or two man in the Nazi hierarchy. When a report was issued it declared the police were in custody of one, Rudolf Hess. The next morning the Duke of Hamilton visited the prisoner, their dialogue later erased.

The last thing Hitler said publicly about Hess was, if he'd only drown in the North Sea then he would vanish without a trace.

Imprisoned in the Tower of London for many of the war years, what he might have said to his captors remains secret. After the war he was flown to Nuremburg where he and other Nazi officials were put on trial for their crimes against humanity. While many were sentenced to death, Hess was given a life sentence. He was transferred to Spandau Prison in Berlin, spending the rest of his life there, eventually becoming the last inmate when others died or were released after serving their sentences. He died on August 17, 1987 and was briefly buried at Wunsiedel Cemetery in Wunsiedel Germany. When his grave site became a holy shrine to neo-Nazis his body was retrieved, sent to a crematorium, his ashes scattered at various locations in the North Sea.